ME & MY DOPE BOY II

SHVONNE LATRICE

Other Works by Me:

Good Girls Love Thugs 1-5
Falling for a Hood King 1-4
Married to a Distinguished Thug 1-3
She's Gotta Have It 1-2
Me & My Dope Boy 1-3
Yazir & Nina 1-3
Forbidden Love with a Thug 1-3
You Needed Me 1-3
Shorty is in Love with a Real One 1-4
I Got Your Back 1-2
My Baby Is a West Coast King 1-4
Our Love Is the Realest 1-3
She Got It Bad for a Heartless Gangsta 1-4
She Got It Bad for a Heartless Gangsta: An AK Christmas
Hood Boyz Fall In Love Too 1-3
Nobody Can Love You Like Them Roughnecks Do 1-4
She Gave Her All to the Hood's Finest 1-5

Visit www.theshvonnelatrice.com for paperbacks!

$15.99
ISBN 978-1-966375-08-1

1 / GIANNA "GIGI" DANIELS

I LOVED this whole cabin thing with KJ. Even better was that we were snowed in! KJ couldn't go anywhere and that shit made me happy as fuck, because I could be all up under him, over him, and on him.

It was around 9pm at night, and it was snowing super heavy outside. You could see the pretty white snow falling down from the window; it was perfect. KJ and I were lying in bed, and he was rubbing my small stomach as we listened to music. I caressed his smooth hair as I slowly rocked my head to the Jazz that filled the room.

"Are you hungry?" he asked me and kissed my belly.

"Of course," I chuckled.

On the way up here, we'd bought a lot of groceries just in case we got snowed in and couldn't leave. We both got out of bed, and put on something to go into the kitchen with. He wore boxers only, and I'd slipped on a little nightgown.

"You want shredded chicken tacos?" I asked and he nodded happily. Tacos were his favorite food, and homemade cinnamon buns were his favorite dessert. I whipped up the food, along with some salsa, and then pulled down the tortilla chips from the cabinet. "Here you go, baby," I said and set the plate in KJ's lap, and then went to get our cups of juice. I sat down next to him with mine, and then we held hands so that we could pray.

"Damn shorty, I'm glad you made me five," he chuckled and bit one.

"There is more stuff in there, so let me know if you want more," I smiled. "The cinnamon buns are cooling right now."

"You tryna get that ring ASAP, huh?" he raised a brow and sipped his juice.

"Not even, I can't cook for my man?" I frowned playfully.

"Nah, you definitely can. And I wasn't saying it like that. I meant you gon' make me give you one on my own," he kissed my face. We scarfed the food down, and then ate some of the cinnamon buns, before making some hot chocolate and cuddling up to watch some TV.

"Gimme a kiss," I said to him after he cut the lamp off, making the room more romantic. He looked down at me, and then kissed me gently before sucking my lips. I cupped his face, and played with his chin hairs as we made love with our mouths.

"I love you, Gianna," he whispered in between kisses and rubbed my stomach.

I climbed onto his lap, straddled him, and then brought the cover over us. We bear hugged and then began kissing hungrily again.

"I love you so much, Kendrick," I whispered back as he caressed my backside. Suddenly, the lights came on, so KJ pushed the covers off of us.

"What the fuck!" he called out when he saw London standing there. He moved me off of his lap, and I just sat there dumbfounded by this old bitch.

"KJ, you can't do this!" she sobbed hysterically. Her mascara was running down her face, but her hair was in perfect condition.

"London, are you fucking crazy?" KJ frowned and stood up. I was frozen in place because I had no idea what the fuck to do.

"KJ, I love you, why can't you see that?" she cried and threw her hands out.

"Yo London, you have to go, shorty. I don't care if it's a blizzard out there," KJ shook his head and started towards her.

"Well if I can't have you," she said and retrieved a gun from her waist.

"No!" I screamed.

POP!

London's brains splattered onto the wall and she slumped to the floor, still holding the gun in her hand. Her head was blown open from the top, and blood dripped down the sides of her face. I stared at her in disbelief, scared that she was still gonna hop up and shoot one of us too. *Did she really just kill herself over KJ? What the fuck kind of relationship did they have?* I wondered. I assumed she was just some freak of the week, but she seemed to think there was more. I mean, there was no way she would kill herself if KJ was just a fuck buddy; not unless she was completely out of her fucking mind. I looked up at KJ who was staring down at her body just as floored as I was. There was complete and utter silence except for the soft Jazz still coming from the bedroom.

"What the fuck man?" he finally sighed and then walked out of the living room.

I didn't wanna be left alone in the living room with this dead bitch, especially because her eyes were wide open as she laid there on the floor. This was like something out of a movie right now. I threw the blanket off of my lap and rushed to catch up to KJ. He grabbed some sheets out of the linen closet, and then he shoved them right back in. I could tell he'd changed whatever plan he'd initially had.

"What are you doing, Kendrick?" I questioned and followed him back out to the living room. He didn't respond and just grabbed the phone. "Kendrick!" I shouted.

"Gianna, just sit down and be quiet baby, okay?" He frowned and gave me the lightest peck on the lips ever.

I rolled my eyes and then went and sat down like he'd asked. He carried the phone with him as he looked out the window.

"The blizzard seems to still be going strong but fuck it," he said. I knew he wasn't talking to me even though he'd said it aloud, so I just rolled my eyes again and folded my arms.

I heard him dial, but he stopped after three numbers, letting me know it was 911 he was calling. I knew it was rare for niggas like KJ to dial 911 so I was confused.

"What are you doing?" I stood up on the couch using my knees.

He hung up and said, "Calling the police. Be quiet, Gianna." He then scoffed like I was irritating every inch of him. I didn't care though because I was just as much a part of this situation as him.

"Why?" I questioned.

"So they can come get this bitch," he turned his lip up as if I was an idiot.

"But–"

"Gianna, I don't know who she told that she was coming up here. If I get rid of her body, and her homegirl or some shit tells the police that the last time she spoke with her was when she was coming to see me, they're gonna come looking for my ass. If I try to tell them that she killed herself, they're gonna wonder why I got rid of the body, and they're not gonna believe me. That will open up a whole new can of worms," he explained to me and raised a brow, waiting for me to confirm that I got the plan.

I nodded because I now understood. Thank God my nigga had brains because I would've been trying to throw her ass into the fireplace or some shit.

"What if they don't believe you?" I frowned.

I really didn't want them to try and arrest my baby. I would bring that bitch back to life and kill her ass again, even if I had to crash her damn funeral to get to her.

"We have cameras, baby," he replied and put a shirt on. "We cut them on whenever this place is visited, and then we remove the tape when we leave. But it's gonna be our evidence today," he added.

"KJ, doesn't that tape show us fucking on it then?" I asked mortified.

"That's definitely on there," he chuckled like something was funny.

"KJ!" I hit the couch with my fist.

"Look, I'm sure you look great on it baby. But would you rather your man go to jail, or just give these policemen a little harmless show?" he inquired seriously. I smacked my lips and then turned my back to him to sit down. "Exactly. The last thing they care about is watching me tear that pussy up, shorty," he snickered, and then I heard him dialing again.

The police were able to get up here with no problem, despite the heavy ass snowfall. Their cars surrounded the place, while all these other people that weren't in uniform surrounded the body. KJ explained what happened, and they requested to see the tape right then.

I was biting my fingernails down to the white meat as I watched them tune in to the living room footage. One of the detectives let out a light chuckle at me getting fucked doggy style on the couch, and then he fast-forwarded for a little until he saw London appear. Re-watching her take her own life made my stomach hurt. It seemed to be more graphic watching it on tape. This shit was really crazy right now.

"And you say this is a woman you were dating?" the detective quizzed KJ.

"Dating, not really. We had a *casual sexual* relationship. She wasn't my girlfriend or anything of that nature," he responded honestly.

"Did *she* know she wasn't your girlfriend?" the detective questioned.

I snapped my neck to look at KJ, because I was wondering the same damn thing. You would've thought KJ was her husband, and I was the mistress with the way this hoe reacted.

"Yes, she knew she wasn't my girlfriend. I explained to her

numerous times that she and I were just having sex. This is my girl-friend right here," KJ tugged me over to him gently. The detective looked at me and gave me a half smile like he was remembering the footage of us on the couch.

"Right," he chuckled and wrote something on his notepad. "Okay, this was a great help young man. Are you two okay?" he asked KJ and me.

"Yeah, we're good, we just wanna get that area cleaned up," KJ nodded and I just gave a half smile, because I was embarrassed and still in shock at the event.

"Of course, my team just wants to get their pictures in and such. There isn't a need to collect much, because the tape says it all," he nodded and put his pale ashy hands on his waistline.

"Cool," KJ nodded.

After about two hours, there were no remnants of London's crazy ass, except for in my mind. The scene just kept replaying in my head, and I didn't know whether I should feel bad or not. What had KJ done to her to make her so crazy? At least if she tried to shoot me that would make more sense, but to feel like she couldn't live without KJ, and she wasn't even his bitch was bananas. This was just fucking with me.

Once every police car and detective car was gone, KJ and I walked to the bathroom. We felt we needed a bath for some reason.

"KJ, are you sure you didn't do anything to make her think you guys were more? I mean, what she just did was pretty over the top to be just a side chick," I said to him.

He folded his sexy arms across his chest and just stared down at me with a blank expression.

"Gigi, everything that you heard me say to that detective is the same shit I said to London, just not as nicely. I never took her out, never spent the night, never told her I loved her, and I never bought her shit, ever. All I gave her was this dick, and nothing more," he responded finally.

"That's it, huh?" I raised a brow.

"Yes woman, damn," he chuckled. "These hoes can't get a taste of good dick without getting attached these days," he said. I just stood there in silence, palming my stomach because I had nothing to say. "You good, shorty?" KJ brought me into his chest.

I wrapped my arms around his torso and just nodded, even though I was shaken up. He pulled away, cupped my face, and pressed his lips against mine. He got down, lifted my nightgown, and then kissed my stomach too.

"Are you alright man?" he chuckled.

"It could be a girl in there!" I smiled at the thought of my baby.

"Nah, I think I only make boys just like my dad," he stood up and walked to the bathtub.

"What about Kendria?" I laughed.

"I don't know how that happened," he laughed as well. "I think it was because my mom prayed for a girl a lot," he cackled and so did I.

"Well, I'm gonna do the same," I said as he turned the water on to start the bath.

"You better not," he said in a low tone as his dark green eyes pierced through me. He walked over to me, lifted my gown over my head, and then slipped his tongue into my mouth.

"I love you, Kendrick," I whispered, and tried to erase the craziness from my mind.

Was my man's dick that good? Or were he and London more than he was letting on?

It was so fucking cold as I walked to my car, and I couldn't wait to blast the heat in my whip. I was leaving the liquor store because I was craving some sweets, candy, and soda. I usually didn't even like soda, but now that I was with child, it was all I wanted to drink. Kaleeini would have to force me to drink water, because otherwise it would not be a part of the equation. I was never the type of girl who loved sweets, but these days I wanted every donut, cupcake, or soda pop I saw. I witnessed someone eat a burger with a split glazed donut as the bun, and I was actually drooling over it; I was not myself.

As I neared my car, I heard tires screech and then a Starbucks coffee cup was thrown at my shoes. Even though freezing outside, the shit still burned my feet through my UGGS. I was pissed as fuck! Not because my feet got slightly burnt, but because my UGGS were somewhat ruined. I loved my hometown, but I hated the dumb ass niggas in it. In some areas, if you weren't getting your shit robbed, your shit was getting ruined, and in this case it was the latter.

"I knew I should've worn the black ones," I said to myself as I hit the alarm on my new 2016 Lexus.

Kaleeini had just bought me this car, and I did not complain. My mother, who was weary of Kaleeini initially because of what he did, now loved him because of this car; power of the moolah. Anyway, it was fully loaded, black, and had leather interior. I picked out all the customs myself, and had it shipped to the dealer.

I slipped into my car, and then cracked open the soda immediately. I downed half of the can before starting my car so I could hurry and get out of West Baltimore. I was going to Kaleeini's house, because just like every day that I was off work, I wanted to spend time with him; and even the days I did have to work. I'd been calling out a lot lately because I always felt tired, clammy, and hungry, so I knew my job security was on its last leg.

Anyways, usually on my days off, Kaleeini and I would go to dinner, the movies, or sometimes chill inside. When I was with Brice, I hated spending all my free time with him, and this was before his illness kicked in. I just didn't feel the need to spend every waking moment with him, but with Kaleeini, I enjoyed his company. I think it was because he and I spent a while unwillingly, building a friendship, so we were straight up homies at the end of the day. Whereas with Brice, he was just my man and nothing else. We never stayed up all night talking or doing anything that Kaleeini and I do besides sex. I could tell Kaleeini anything and then fuck him afterward, so it was the best of both worlds.

About thirty minutes later, because of traffic, I arrived at Kaleeini's home in Federal Hill. I typed the code into the remote, and then hit open so his gates would let me in. I did the same for the garage, and then used my key to get inside this mansion.

Yes bitches, I had a key, and I flaunted it. I went to Lowe's and had them make the key with a Minnie Mouse design and everything. I preferred this house to my small condo with my mom anyway. And I loved that he would allow me to come and go as I pleased, even when he wasn't home.

I walked in and went straight to the kitchen to put up the snacks that I wasn't gonna eat right now. I'd just restocked Kaleeini's fridge because I enjoyed cooking meals for him whenever I was over here. His mom, Morgan loved that about me, she said. She told me she could take a break now because Kaleeini always needed her or he would starve. I was happy to take the load off of her though. I laughed to myself as I closed the cabinet.

I heard Kaleeini yelling, so I knew his ass was playing his fucking video game. I walked to his game room, and there he was sitting on the couch looking as fine as ever. He had on basketball shorts, boxers, and socks. His dreads swept his strong shoulders, as he played his video game with so much passion that his six-pack flexed with every move. I plopped down next to him and played with his dreads. He ignored me until he finished his session, and then put the controller down to kiss me.

"Hey beautiful, how are my two babies?" he grinned, and his green eyes sparkled brightly.

"They're doing just fine, especially since they've had some grape soda," I laughed and then he tickled me making me scream.

"I told you to ease up on that shit," he chuckled.

"I know, I only had one."

"What the fuck happened to your shoes shorty?"

"Oh, some dumb niggas threw coffee on them," I shrugged.

"What? Just randomly?"

"Yeah. They were just some random niggas being stupid. It was over in West Baltimore, they have all the best liquor stores over there."

"Nah, that don't sound right," he shook his head and pursed his sexy lips like he was thinking.

"What you mean?"

"I just can't see some people randomly throwing coffee on your feet like that," he squinted his eyes and stared off. "I be over on the Westside a lot and ain't no niggas ever done no shit like that to me."

"Because you're a big tall ass nigga with dreads and I'm not. It's the hood, people do ignorant shit all the time," I said and removed my boots.

"I want you to live with me, shorty. I need to keep a better eye on you," he looked at me. "And by the way, there are plenty of liquor stores around South Baltimore."

"Kaleeini, I'm fine. I promise it was nothing," I chuckled, but he was obviously serious since he didn't crack a smile. "And I don't like these uppity ass liquor stores down here," I pouted.

"Well, either way, I'm gonna hire someone to watch you."

"Fine, I will move in," I shook my head and smacked my lips as if I didn't want to. Shit, I'd been waiting on this shit.

"Don't be acting like I'm twisting your arm, shorty. You know you're happy about getting all day access to this dick here," he nudged me.

"Whatever you say," I half smiled.

"I know it's whatever I say," he leaned in and started to suck my lips.

Living here was about to be a full on party, and I couldn't wait.

I woke next to my beautiful fiancée, and smiled as I thought about the night I proposed. She was so happy, and that in turn made me happy. I wanted Willow to know that I loved her more than anything, and that she didn't need to fight so hard for me anymore. She'd been on her best behavior though, and I was happy about that. I was so tired of pulling her off of these hoes.

I stared at her and she stirred a little bit but stayed asleep. She was naked, so I kissed on her back a couple times before laying her on it. I dipped down under the covers, placed her smooth light cinnamon colored thighs on my shoulders, and pecked her lower lips. I ran my tongue between the slit, and then began sucking on her clit. She moved a little bit, and then I finally felt her lift the covers off my head a little.

"Kendrin, are you serious right now? Mmm, aahhh," she moaned loudly.

She hit the area next to her with her fist, just as I pushed her thighs towards her stomach to kill it. I was sucking and licking her so ferociously, that I thought she was gonna pass out.

"Aahhh, aahhh, oh my fuck!" She couldn't even complete her sentences as I feasted on her.

"Oh, oh, I'm about to cum so hard, oh my gosh!" she called out in a high-pitched voice as her nails scraped the sheets. "Ahhhh!" she whimpered as she released her juices. I tried to keep going but she pushed my head away making me laugh. "I feel like I need to pay you for that," she giggled, still panting heavily.

I kissed her trembling thighs, and then up her stomach. She pulled me up then slipped her tongue into my mouth.

"See how good you taste," I said, and she licked her lips with a lustful look in her eyes. I pecked her again then pushed my dick inside of her.

"Ah," she jumped a little and then bit down on her lip.

I lifted her legs into the nook of my arms, and then placed my hands against the headboard to lock her in. She couldn't move anywhere even if she tried.

"I hate you, mmm," she pursed her lips as I stroked her slowly and in a circular motion.

I pulled out slowly, and went inside fast. She put her hands against my abs and rubbed them gently. We stared each other in the eyes as I got her used to my size, and that shit was feeling too good. I looked down between her legs and saw she was juicing up nicely, so it was time for me to beat it up.

"Shit, I'm cumming again," her chest heaved up and down before she let loose on my rod.

Once she came I started going ham. Because I had her legs locked in the nook of my arms, she had no choice but to take the dick.

"Ahh, aahhh, ahhh, Kendrin, aahhh!" she yelled as I slammed into her constantly.

Damn this was some good pussy. It was so good I couldn't even say anything aloud. Right now, I had to stay in communication with my dick so I wouldn't nut just yet.

"Babyyy, fuck, ahh, ahhh, ahhh," she scrunched up her beautiful face and tried to move away, but like I said—she had nowhere to run.

"Shit Lo, I'm about to nut," I grunted as I felt her explode again.

Seeing her naked body, and the way my dick pulverized her pussy was too much for me.

"Give me that nut, daddy," she whimpered and I shot up the club immediately after.

"Oh fuck," I panted as she rubbed up and down my six-pack. That nut took every damn thing out of me it seemed.

"And you wonder why I be trying to beat bitches up," she attempted to catch her breath. I just chuckled at her, and then kissed her again.

After that fuck session, we both showered and got dressed. I came downstairs after making some phone calls, to some pancakes, eggs, and pepper bacon.

"Smells good," I smiled and sat at the island in my kitchen.

"So, I made an appointment to taste some cakes. It's two weeks from now," she said and set my plate in front of me.

She held up some orange juice and I nodded to say I wanted some. "Baby, I thought you wanted to get married in the summer, it's still winter," I frowned.

"True, but the girl that I want a cake from needs six months in advance. So if we get married in June, I need to order now," she responded.

"Six months? How long does it take to make a fucking cake? That shit better be fresh," I scoffed and ate my pancakes.

"Baby, it's gonna be fresh. She's just a very busy woman because people order cakes from her constantly," Willow laughed at me and I just shook my head.

"So what, I gotta come to this shit?" I frowned.

I didn't feel like dealing with a fucking wedding. Women liked that shit so why not do it alone? Just tell me how much the shit costs so I can pay, and we're good.

"Don't you wanna know what our wedding cake will taste like?" She sat next to me to eat her food.

"Not really. As long as it's not red velvet, because that shit is over-rated, I'm okay with it," I turned my lip up. "Just tell me where and when we're getting married, and I will show up," I laughed and she shot daggers at me.

"Kendrin, no, we need to be equal partners," she whined.

"I get that baby, but I don't wanna cake taste. That's for metro-sexual niggas," I responded and she laughed.

"Fine, I will ask my friends to come, you brat."

"Thanks, I love you," I kissed her neck which smelled like sweet perfume.

"Me too," she said dryly.

"Nah, I need better than that," I said in a low tone as I kissed her chin.

"I love you too, daddy," she grinned and I pecked her soft lips.

"Much better."

I WAS WALKING *into the gym for another crazy ass, strenuous practice, when I heard my phone going off in my pocket. I reached in and retrieved it right when the ringing stopped, and I saw Shannon had called me ten times. Usually I would call her after practice, but the amount of times she called me alarmed me. I dropped my bag in the lobby area of the gym, and dialed her back.*

"Kenzie, you need to get over here!" she shouted as soon as she picked up. I heard ambulance sirens in the back, and Shannon was frantic as hell. I was worried as fuck.

"What happened babe?" I quizzed as I darted back out to the parking lot to leave. I didn't have time to let my coach know anything. I would have to call him later because Shannon came first.

"Just get over here to my apartment now," she smacked her lips and hung up in my face.

She sounded scared yet angry, so I had no idea what was actually going on. I sped to her apartment and got there in about twenty minutes. I exited my car, and rushed over to see why the ambulance was here, since she gave me no info over the phone.

As I neared Shannon's apartment building, I saw Rosalind on a stretcher crying and screaming. I knew this was bad, I thought.

What the fuck is Rosalind doing over here? Does Shannon know about us now? I wondered to myself as I watched them roll Rosalind away. Although not my girl anymore, I had to know what was up.

I ran over to the EMT and asked, "What the hell happened to her?" I'd realized that Rosalind was bleeding at the bottom of her skirt, and my stomach dropped. My baby, I said to myself.

"Who are you?" the EMT sized me up like she wanted to fight.

"I-I'm her... umm, I'm her baby's father," I responded and looked over my shoulder when I heard footsteps. Shannon was standing behind me crying and shaking her head. Fuck, if she didn't know before, she sure in the fuck knew now.

"She may have miscarried. You can't ride but you can follow to Saint Agnes Hospital," the EMT said and then ran around to drive off.

I nodded even though she wasn't looking, and then turned to face Shannon. I started to walk closer to her so that I could hold her and console her.

WHAM!

She slapped me, and when I was about to recover she started taking off on me.

"Shannon! Shannon! Baby, stop!" I hollered as I tried to grab ahold of her.

"You fucking lying ass nigga!" she screamed. I felt her tears hit my forearms as I grabbed her wrists to restrain her. "I hate you Kenzie! How could you do this!" she shouted once I got her fast ass fists under control. Got damn, where did she learn to swing like this?

"Shannon, baby, I'm sorry," I panted and bear hugged her so she couldn't leave or hit me again.

"I loved you Kenzie, how could you!" she sobbed violently into my chest.

"Shannon, come to my house with me so I can talk to you," I said calmly and pulled away.

"There ain't shit to talk about. Good luck with your baby mama," she hissed and then ran away towards her apartment. I chased her and

scooped her ass up as she screamed and kicked for me to let her go. Her father ran out and down the stairs to see the ruckus.

"Kenzie, let her go!" he demanded. I really didn't want to, but I knew this situation was about to get out of hand. "Let her go Kenzie," her father repeated in a calmer tone as he tried to peel my hands from Shannon's waist.

By now, Shannon had given up fighting me off her, and was using all of her strength to cry. I let her go, and her father had to carry her bridal style up the stairs, because her limbs were like noodles. Watching that shit was heart wrenching like a muthafucka.

Defeated, I watched them until they disappeared into the apartment, and then I went to the car so I could go visit Rosalind. Regardless of who was my girl and who wasn't, my baby was in danger. As I cranked my car up, my coach's name flashed across my phone. I didn't feel like dealing with his loud crazy ass, but I knew I had to.

"Hello," I answered and sighed.

"King, where are you?" he questioned angrily. We had a big game coming up, so every practice was pivotal at this point.

"Man, I have a family issue, I can't make it," I huffed and ran my hand over my face.

"That's thirty laps from you," he spat.

"I know, I got you," I responded before hanging up. I didn't wanna hear his damn voice anymore. "Fuck!" I hollered before pulling from the curb.

That day kept replaying in my head over and over. I was sitting in my room thinking about Shannon, Rosalind, and the baby that was no longer. I kept picturing all the blood that was all over Rosalind's clothes, and how she cried like a newborn baby when they said the baby was gone. I felt bad for breaking up with her, even though her ass had cheated. Maybe if I hadn't have neglected her so much, she wouldn't have run to another nigga, who happened to be my cousin. I should've been honest with her about Shannon from the get go, and none of this would be happening right now. I was the worst nigga at the moment, and the feeling was terrible.

I sipped the bottle of water sitting on my nightstand, and then grabbed my phone to call Shannon. She hadn't been answering, and I was losing it. Every text, call, and social media message I sent went unanswered. I even lurked around her classes to see if I could bump into her, but somehow I never saw her. I was missing her like crazy, and I didn't know what to do to get her to see me or talk to me.

As far as Rosalind, she was off me too. I think losing the baby hardened her heart, because once they told her, she screamed for me to leave the hospital and never talk to her again. I saw it in her eyes that she hated me, and honestly how could I blame her? I knew a miscarriage was scarring to a woman, and she wouldn't have had this horrible memory if I hadn't been trying to be man of the year to two different women.

On top of all this, I barely had time to sit and think because I was always practicing on my game. I knew I couldn't allow all this personal shit to interfere with my goals in life, but damn was it fucking hard.

KNOCK!

KNOCK!

"Come in!" I called out and fell backwards on my bed. My mother walked in with a tray of food, but I wasn't too hungry.

"You want some breakfast?" she half smiled.

"I'm good, Ma," I responded dryly.

My mother was furious when I told her what happened, but when I said the baby died she wasn't as angry with me. She felt bad and wanted to see Rosalind, but I let her know that she hated me and told me to never speak to or see her again. My father really didn't have any words for me, I guess because he too had a baby by another woman, and wasn't in the place to judge. My sister Kennedy was born to some heroin addict stripper that my dad got caught up with. She was my sister though, regardless of who her mother was.

"Kenzie, it's gonna be okay. You just have to give it time," my mom sat next to me and I sat up.

"Give which situation time? The baby or Shannon?" I frowned.

I may not have carried the child, but knowing my mistakes killed my own offspring before it had a chance to breathe air cut me deep.

"Both, especially Shannon, baby. This just happened yesterday afternoon, what do you expect from her?" She rubbed my back.

"I don't know, Ma, I expect her to forgive me I guess," I shrugged and she chuckled.

"Maybe she will, but calling her all day is not gonna do it. You really messed up Kenzie, so if she does forgive you, which she may not, it's gonna take some time," she said.

"She may not? She has to forgive me. If she doesn't then she never loved me," I shook my head and stared at the floor.

"That's unfair, Kenzie. She could say the same thing about you. The fact that you had a girlfriend who *I* didn't even know about, and you got her pregnant, one could say that you didn't love Shannon or you wouldn't have done that," she explained.

She was right but I didn't want her to be. I wanted Shannon to be obligated to forgive me, because a part of me felt like she never would. The thought alone made me physically sick. I didn't know what I would do without Shannon. No other girl would be able to fill her shoes, and I would be ill if I saw another nigga trying to fill mine with her.

"But eat your food. How are you gonna make it to the NBA if you're malnourished?" my mom kissed my face and caressed my short curly hair. I grabbed the tray that she'd set down, and then began to dig in. "I love you, Kenzie," she said and kissed me again.

"I love you too, Ma," I exhaled and ate some more, as she got up and exited my room. Fuck my life.

I CALLED Shannon earlier because she missed our nail appointment yesterday, and hadn't returned any of my texts either. It was odd because we'd just talked that morning, and she said that after class she would be going straight to the nail shop. I called Aysia to see if she had talked to her, but she said she text her and got no response like me. I knew Gianna hadn't seen her, since she was currently away at the cabin, but she said that Shannon hadn't replied to any of her texts as well. Gianna also said she had some shit to tell us, and I couldn't wait until she got back in a couple days. I begged her to tell me over the phone, but she said we all needed to be face to face.

I pulled up to Shannon's apartment because I was worried about her. The four of us never ignored each other's texts. Even when we were mad, we always answered. We'd made a pact long ago to always answer no matter what, so that we knew everyone was okay. So the fact that she wasn't replying was beyond odd.

I got out and went inside the apartment building, and then went up the stairs to Shannon's door. I knocked on it, and her father answered shortly after.

"Oh, hi Willow," he half smiled. He looked tired and very worried, which made my heart beat fast.

"Hi Mr. Breaux, is Shannon in?" I asked even though I knew she was. Her car was parked outside, and Kendrin was over Kenzie's house so I knew she wasn't with him.

He looked over his shoulder, paused, and said, "Yeah come in."

Mr. Breaux had always been a nice guy, but I hoped he wasn't up to any bullshit. He was acting kind of suspiciously, like he didn't want me to see Shannon. I followed him to her room, and he knocked lightly with his knuckles.

"Dad, please leave me alone," Shannon cried out, and I jerked my neck back. Why the hell was she crying? Shannon was tough, so for her to cry it had to have been bad.

"You wanna try?" he pointed to her door and I nodded. He went to his room, and closed the door behind him.

I knocked lightly just as Mr. Breaux had done prior, but before Shannon could respond, I twisted the knob to go in.

"Dad-" she turned over but stopped talking when she saw me.

She was wearing a t-shirt and panties, with her hair hanging down. Her smooth brown skin looked flushed, and I could tell that whatever had happened really hurt her deeply.

"Willow," she whispered and wiped her cheek with the back of her hand, as I shut and locked the door.

"Shan, what's wrong?" I squinted my eyes and sat next to her.

"Kenzie cheated on me," she sobbed by putting her face into her hands. Her body jerked, and she was struggling to breathe a little.

"Kenzie?" I frowned in confusion.

Kenzie was in love with Shannon, so to hear that he cheated was downright unbelievable.

"Yes, he had another girlfriend who he's been with for years, and they were having a baby," she sobbed harder.

I felt like I was in a dream, because we couldn't have been talking about the same Kenzie. This nigga would take a bullet for Shannon, and worshipped the ground that she walked on. I can't even see how another woman could convince Kenzie to pull his dick out of his pants. Also, Kendrin never mentioned Kenzie being in a relationship with someone else before he and Shannon got together, and I was with Kendrin way before they dated. Kenzie was a single guy from what I understood, so I had no idea where this girlfriend of years came from.

"Wait, who told you this?" I asked.

"The girl, and Kenzie himself. It happened yesterday and she approached me. And then I think she lost the baby when I pushed her," she looked into my face with worried eyes.

"Wait, what?" I frowned up.

"When she came to approach me, she grabbed my arm to stop me from leaving. I tried to just pull my arm from her grasp, but I instead made her lose her balance and fall down the hallway stairs," Shannon explained. "Blood was everywhere, and she was just screaming calling me a murderer," she began to sob heavily again.

My mind was blown right now, because how did so much transpire in a matter of twenty-four damn hours? The last time I saw Shannon and Kenzie, they were damn near about to fuck in front of me. So how was it that now he was with someone else and having a baby, who was now no longer, at the hands of Shannon? My brain was hurting right now.

"Kenzie admitted to this-"

I was cut off by the sound of her phone buzzing. I looked down and it was Kenzie.

"I wish he would leave me alone!" she grunted. I picked up her phone, and she shook her head no so I wouldn't answer it. I hit decline, and then set it back down.

"He admitted this Shannon?" I finished my question and she nodded. I knew she said he admitted it, but I needed to hear it twice to be sure.

"I'm so angry and I'm so miserable, Lo," she cried violently. "How did this happen to me? How did I not know he had another girl?" she shook her head and sniffled.

"I don't think anyone could have sensed it, Shan. He was with you every hour that he wasn't in practice. How did he even have time to make the baby?" I chuckled very lightly trying to make her feel better.

"I should've listened to Kendria," she cried.

"What did she say?" I furrowed my brows.

"She told me she overheard some girl saying that Kenzie was her sister's boyfriend! I was suspicious, but that lying ass nigga convinced me that it was just hearsay," she smacked her lips and snatched a Kleenex from the box. "I'm sure it was that baby mama's sister that Kendria overheard," she added after wiping her nose.

Where the hell have I been? In a damn cave or some shit? I feel like I fell asleep for a week or some shit with all this information she was dropping on me.

"Damn," was all I could say as I looked down at her beige carpet.

"I feel sick," she bit her bottom lip as more tears gushed from her big brown eyes.

"I'm so sorry, boo." I didn't know what else to say, so I just hugged her. I felt so bad as her body jerked against mine.

"I love him so much and I wish I didn't anymore," she wept.

"I know, but we seem to fall in love quicker than we fall out," I said while rubbing her back. She didn't say anything else, and just cried as if her life was over.

I stayed with Shannon for a little longer, until Aysia came to take over. When I explained everything to her, because Shannon was too much of a mess to retell it again, she was just as perplexed as I. No one saw this coming, and I think it made both Aysia and I look at our niggas sideways too, unfortunately. Shit, these niggas *were* related.

As soon as I left, I picked up some Starbucks for myself, and then went home so I could relax. I felt so bad for Shannon, and I was still floored at the same time. If you would have seen the way Kenzie looked at Shannon, and the way he talked to and about her, you would be just as surprised as I. Something just wouldn't allow me to think he was just putting up a front the whole time. There had to be a better explanation, because if all niggas treated their side chicks the way Kenzie treated Shannon, there would be way more of them than there are now.

I walked into my house, and went upstairs to start my bath with one of my new bath bombs. When I entered the bedroom, I saw Kendrin sitting on the bed texting, and he put his phone away when he saw me.

"Did you know?" I immediately asked him and he nodded slowly, clearly knowing what I was talking about.

"Why didn't you tell me?" I frowned.

"For what, Lo? That's not my place. That's between Shannon and Kenzie," he said.

"Whatever, all y'all niggas stick together," I waved him off and went to the bathroom. He was right on my heels, and grabbed my arm so I could face him. "Move, Kendrin." I tried to pull my arm back but he had a good grip on it.

"Aye look, I know that's your friend, but that's my cousin. On top of that, the only thing you should be worried about is me, and all I'm worried about is you. There is no reason that we should be mad at each other over someone else's relationship," he kissed me gently. "Okay?" He hunched his back a little so that he could look into my eyes, and I nodded.

"I'm sorry, it's just I hate seeing her cry like that. I've never see her so sad," I sighed and turned the bath water on. This shit had me wondering if Kendrin had a baby mama tucked away somewhere.

"I know, and Kenzie isn't exactly over at the crib doing the Harlem Shake shorty," he replied and I chuckled.

"I know; I just didn't see this coming. They were so in love."

"They still are in love, just give it time," he pulled me back over to him. "Plus, that bitch is probably lying again."

"Again? What do you mean?" I frowned.

"Kenzie's supposed baby mama is the same bitch that told you *I* was her baby daddy," he explained and my jaw dropped.

"Wait, the same hoe that told me she was pregnant by you, is Kenzie's girlfriend of *years*?" I questioned and used air quotes when saying years. Kendrin nodded and shrugged. "Wow, what the hell!" I turned my nose up.

"It's crazy but stay out of it Lo. I don't want you in the middle of nothing, aight shorty?" he raised his brow. "Aight?" he chuckled because I was just staring at him, not wanting to agree.

"Fine! Wanna watch a movie when I get out?" I leaned my head back to look up into his face.

"Yes, but are you cooking?" he inquired.

"Order pizza," I grinned and he kissed me passionately.

As fucked up as it may sound, I was happy as hell me and my nigga were good... from what I knew.

It'd been three days since my heart got broken, and it didn't seem to be getting any better. I was so confused, and every day I prayed to wake up so that all of this would be just a horrible nightmare. But every single morning, I saw that this pain was all too real. It hurt physically to think about what had happened to my relationship in just a matter of hours. My head throbbed constantly, and my stomach felt queasy.

Kenzie didn't call me at all for the past two days, but today he'd been blowing me up again with texts too. I missed him but I couldn't let that cancel out my pride. I didn't want my love for him to allow him to walk all over me. I would rather die than be some side chick who has to stay in her place. Even though I loved Kenzie, I couldn't be his side hoe or any other nigga's for that matter.

I just don't understand why he did this to me. He claimed he loved me so much, yet he had me as his mistress for over a year. I don't even know how he was able to pull the shit off, because like Willow said, he was always with me. There was never a time when he didn't answer his phone or anything like that. Then again, he was pretty adamant about me not surprising him in Virginia, and I guess now I know why. The thought alone made my stomach drop. He was probably laid up with her just like he was with me when I visited. Ugh!

Shit, if you think about it, I guess Rosalind is the one that should be the angriest, because she was his girl first, and he just added me to the equation. I shook my head as I made my way through the parking lot of the school. I just wanted to go home and cry some more.

As I was walking, I felt someone grab my arm, and I turned to see Kenzie. I knew he would run up on me at school sooner or later, but I didn't think it'd be this soon. I was hoping it happened when I was feeling stronger and able to brush him off with ease. Now was the worst time, because I was missing him more than ever, and I knew I didn't have the strength to diss him like I wanted and needed to.

"Don't touch me," I glared at him and took my arm from him.

"Shannon, please let me explain myself," he pleaded with prayer hands.

I looked off to the side, and the cold air blew my hair into my face. It dried the tears that were threatening to fall, and I was thankful for that. He moved the hair from my face, and rubbed my cheek with his thumb. I closed my eyes to bask in the moment because I missed his touch. I was used to being in his presence and his arms on a daily basis.

"Just ten minutes," he said in a low tone, and kissed the corner of my mouth. I almost burst into tears at the feeling of his lips against mine.

I nodded to say okay, and he took my hand into his to lead me to his car. He opened the passenger door for me, and then closed it once I was in. I kept my books close to my chest, as I waited for him to get in the car. I was using my books as some sort of armor against this man, because I couldn't fight him off alone.

"It's cold as hell," he chuckled and I ignored him. "Okay Shannon, first off I want you to know that I love you and that every conversation we had, and every time I looked into your eyes and said I loved you more than anything, it was all real," he said and tears started to stroll down my cheeks. I couldn't hold them in anymore. I sniffled and then wiped them as I stared straight ahead. He turned me to face him using my chin, and I admired his sexy caramel face and deep green eyes. "I met Rosalind before you, and yes, she was my girlfriend when I pursued you. I wanted to resist you but I couldn't. Then we fell in love unexpectedly, and I didn't know what to do. I wanted to leave Rosalind and be with you, but I felt like I owed her. I felt bad that I went out and fell in love with someone else while I had a woman at home," he placed his hand on his chest as I started to cry more.

"Kenzie, I can't be your side chick," I sobbed.

"Baby, you were never the side, that's why I was always with you. If anything you were the main. Yeah, she was here first, but I never loved her. I cared for her but I was- I *am* in love with you," he caressed my face and then pressed his lips against mine.

"I love you too," I whispered.

"And I'm sorry baby, I will never hurt you like this ever. This shit was not supposed to happen like this. I broke up with her about a week ago," he explained.

"You got her pregnant, Kenzie! How could you! You don't even care about my health, going around fucking other girls raw and then sticking that same dick inside me!" I hollered at the thought. I was so repulsed by him at the moment.

"Shannon, I never fucked nobody raw but you!" He frowned as if I had him overly fucked up.

"Yeah right! How did she get pregnant then?" I scowled. I was gonna throw up at the thought of sucking his dick after he fucked her with no hat. I hated him right now, and there was nothing he could do to change that!

"I wish I could tell you baby, but I wondered the same thing," he shrugged.

"Well, I appreciate the explanation Kenzie, and good luck on your future," I pulled on the lever to open his door.

"Wait, good luck? The fuck you mean good luck, Shannon? I'm

all for giving you some time, but you gon' leave me?" He furrowed his brows as he held onto my arm.

"Kenzie, what you did was unforgivable, I'm sorry. You and I just need to move on," I said and tried to pull away, but he wouldn't let me. "Let me go, Kenzie," I pulled again, and he yanked me back into the car, before reaching across me to close the door back.

"Shannon, come on baby," he grabbed my face and kissed me hungrily. My body accepted the kiss before my mind could tell me not to.

"Kenzie," I whimpered in between us kissing.

He unbuttoned my coat, and reached under my shirt to squeeze my boob. He then unbuttoned my pants, and he slipped his hand down between my legs.

"I love you, Shan," he whispered as he quickly pushed two fingers inside me. Why was I so weak for this man?

"Ahh, ahh," I moaned into his mouth, as he continued to tongue me down. I hadn't felt him in days, and the feeling right now was mind blowing.

"You love me?" he questioned as he finger fucked me harder.

"Ye-yes, I love you," I stammered as he hit my spot with every finger thrust. "Uugghhh," I grunted softly as I let my juices cover his fingers. He licked them off, and then we kissed again.

"You forgive me?" He looked into my eyes. I nodded my head yes, but I wasn't too sure.

The most beautiful smile covered his gorgeous face, and he slipped his tongue back into my mouth.

I was finally back from the little trip with Gianna, and my mind was still trying to process what London had done. I knew she was tripping over me cutting ties with her, but damn! She had me questioning all the shit that I'd told *her* and the many other bitches I fucked with as well. I couldn't have this shit becoming a fucking habit, because it was mind-boggling. Yes, I had pushed more than a couple wigs back, but seeing someone I had spent time with and interacted with blow their head open was straight crazy. I really had no idea that she felt that deeply for me, and honestly I didn't know how or why. I never spent time with her unless my dick was in her mouth, so I wasn't too sure how she came to feel so strongly for me. Yeah, I told her she could meet my mom, but that wasn't enough for her to be acting out like she was. I racked my brain constantly, trying to see if I led her on in any way, other than the mama shit, but nothing came up. I wanted to just chuck it up to her being crazy, but London wasn't the crazy type. At least she wasn't crazy until I told her I wouldn't be in her life anymore. Outside of that though, she was very sane, and even had her shit together. That's exactly another reason why I had the police handle that shit, because anybody that knew London would've never believed that she killed herself, especially over me. Shit, I wouldn't even have believed it had I not been right there to witness it.

Anyhow, after London took her fucking life, I didn't want to end the trip right away, because the snow was still pretty high and because I promised my girl a trip. I wasn't gonna let London ruin it because she wanted to kill her fucking self. Yeah it was fucked up that she died, but shit she did it to herself, so why should Gianna have to suffer the consequences?

Speaking of Gianna, I could tell my shorty was shaken the fuck up over the suicide, but she did her best to continue to enjoy our little time together. I knew she was wondering if London was more to me than I said, but I assured her that she was nothing more than someone I talked to in order to bust a nut. I hated to speak that way about her now that she was dead, but that was the honest to God truth. And lately, she'd been some last resort pussy, meaning if I was too lazy to grab a new girl to fuck, only then would I hit her up.

I walked through the foyer of my parents' house, and went straight to the den where I found my dad. He'd found out that the police had come up to the cabin, and he was furious. My dad hadn't cursed my ass out in years, so it was still shocking to hear his ass going in on me over the phone. I knew if I was in his presence that we probably would've been throwing fists, because that's how irate this nigga was. I literally had to hold the phone from my ear. He only calmed down when I told him that it had nothing to do with the operation, nor was it because of me being reckless... in a way. Gianna listened in on the call with her eyes bucked, and swore up and down that my dad was gonna murder us. I told her he loved my mom too much to murder me, but I didn't know about her. I was joking but she was still scared as fuck. Ha ha.

"What's up?" I said when I entered, and he gave me a head nod before muting the television.

I was wondering if he was still as furious before. I hoped not, because I was not in the mood to be called anymore dumb ass niggas, or asked does my brain work. Ha ha.

"So what happened up there?" he turned to me. *Cool, this nigga is calm*, I thought.

"Oh my gosh," I ran my hands over my face. "So you know the chick that mom despises?" I looked at him and he nodded. "She somehow got inside the cabin, and straight blew her damn brains out, right there in the living room," I finished and his eyes were bucked.

"Huh? For what?" he furrowed his brows. I knew he was hoping she had a legit excuse for killing herself, but was there really any legit excuse for such an act?

"Because I wouldn't be with her," I shook my head. He squinted his eyes, and I nodded to let him know that dead ass was the reason.

"Wow, I'm used to chicks trying to set you up, but killing themselves? She's old enough to be your damn mama," he scoffed. "What did the police say?" he quizzed.

"I let them watch the tape, and they just thanked me and said that was all the evidence they needed," I replied.

"I see. Well good job because you don't know who she told that she was coming to see you," he patted my back.

"That's exactly why I didn't get rid of her ass myself. If I'm gonna go down for some shit, I want it to at least be something I actually did," I sighed.

"Exactly, and even then you still wanna fight that shit," he said and twisted the cap off of the bottle of water next to him.

"That shit makes me wanna be with one woman for the rest of my life," I exhaled. "I can't have bitches killing themselves on me every damn month."

"Ain't that the plan with Gianna? Especially now that you guys have a baby coming," he inquired.

"Yeah, of course," I smirked. *That is the plan. That is the plan nigga! Don't fuck up the plan KJ!* I chanted to myself.

"KJ, don't make the same mistakes I made. Please do not," he chuckled and set his water bottle down.

"What you mean?" I jerked my neck because I had no idea he had done anything with anybody outside of my mother.

I vaguely remember them breaking up when I was younger, but I had no idea why. I just remember him moving out, and he and my mom being mean to one another. I thought they divorced, but my dad told me that they were married still, so a nigga was confused as hell. Then next thing I know, her belly started getting big and he was living with us again. Ever since then, I'd been calling the baby in her stomach, Kendrae, the break baby.

Seeing my mom pregnant was the scariest shit in the world to me as a kid, because I thought she was sick or something. It was the first time I'd witnessed her being pregnant, because I was only like one and a half when Kendrin was born. When she told me a baby was in there, a nigga was floored as fuck. I cried for days until she told me that once the baby got here she would look normal again. That was just a traumatizing ass year for a young buck, haha. When she got pregnant again with Kendria, I was prepared like a muthafucka. I told all my homies that once she got here, I couldn't play outside because I had to take care of her. I had niggas in the hood thinking my dad had ditched my mom. I don't know what the fuck my seven-year-old ass was talking about.

"What I'm saying is that I've been young, rich, and frisky like you, and it doesn't mix well with love," he replied snapping me from my thoughts. I never knew why my parents broke up, but now I was very interested to find out.

"You cheated before?" my jaw dropped.

"Yes, I've cheated before. I've been messing with women since I was fourteen," he smirked.

"Yeah, I've liked pussy since I was in preschool," I admitted and we both laughed.

It was true though. In preschool, the teacher's aid was this older guy in like ninth grade. And I remember I had to use the bathroom during naptime, and when I came back he was watching porn on his phone. I saw that shit and knew where I wanted to be for the rest of my life. I couldn't wait to grow up so I could be like the nigga in that porno. I don't know why I didn't put two and two together, and figure out that my dad was not in the room tickling my mom. A kid's dumb mind I guess.

"But answer the question, Dad. I know you've cheated on women before, but I'm asking about mom specifically," I looked at him and waited with bated breath.

"Yeah, but it was like early as hell. I did twice, but the first time was the worst ever," he nodded and I was very surprised to hear this.

It was good to know he wasn't perfect though, but I just wished he were imperfect with someone else, because my mom deserved the world. It bothered me a little to hear this, but I'm glad it was a long time ago.

"Why was it the worst?" I inquired although I was scared to know. I didn't want this information to cause me to have ill feelings towards my father. I doubt it would, but you never know.

"Because it was just the wrong time. She was young, she'd just had a baby, and she just came from a situation like that so it just wasn't good," he shook his head and sipped his water. *Damn*, I thought.

"I'm guessing I was the baby," I said and he nodded. "Dang," I exhaled and stared at the bookshelf.

"Then after that she always thought I was cheating in the back of her mind, and the trust just wasn't there. But the important thing is that I learned my lesson eventually," he explained and chuckled.

"How? I love Gianna but it's hard sometimes. I see naked women all the time, and it's difficult to turn these chicks down," I told him. I wanted to learn my lesson; I needed to before I lost Gianna.

I owned a strip club, so women were everywhere and always throwing themselves at me. And these weren't no busted ass bitches either, they looked good as hell. Then I traveled a lot, so bitches from foreign countries were willing to do whatever and whenever. I'd become accustomed to just being able to fuck whenever I wanted, so having to discipline myself was new to me. Why was this shit so hard?

"Well," he set his drink down. "I learned my lesson when she left me. No matter what I did she always forgave me, so when she actually left me it kind of made me see what I had in her," he said. "I always loved your mother, but I kind of took her for granted because she was always willing to forgive me for any and everything. I felt invincible until she bounced. I worried about losing everything else but her, until I lost her. She was something I never thought twice about losing, and that wasn't good because I would sometimes put her last because I knew she wasn't going anywhere. During the time apart I hated it, but in hindsight I think it was good for us," he added.

"What did you do to make her leave?" I quizzed.

"Funny enough, the time she left I was actually innocent, but because I had fucked up so much before, she didn't trust me so," he shrugged.

"Shit," I shook my head. I was not trying to be in that position. The way my parents acted you would never know. My mom didn't treat him like he was a cheater or nothing. She acted as if he was the greatest husband on Earth. "She doesn't even say anything about it," I chuckled.

"That's a part of forgiveness, not throwing it in the person's face all the time. But that's what I love about your mother, she loves me no matter what and she always will."

I talked to my father for a little bit more, and then I went upstairs to see my mom. I walked into the little office she had, and stood in the doorway as I watched her file things. She wore a tight black dress that had no sleeves. She was barefoot, and as always her feet were done.

"What I tell you about those tight dresses?" I laughed and walked into the office. She giggled and then reached up to grab my face and kiss my cheek. "What you doing?" I asked and sat down on the mini couch.

"I am organizing some things so I won't have to search high and low for one little thing," she smiled and pushed her long dark hair behind her ears. "I didn't know you were here baby," she squinted her eyes as I stood back up.

"Oh, I was down there with dad," I pointed over my shoulder and she nodded. "I just came to tell you that I love you, and I'm blessed to have you as my mother," I told her. She looked up at me with her mouth slightly open. I knew when women got cheated on it made them feel like less, and I wanted my mother to know that was not the case with her.

"What brought this on?" she grinned.

"Nothing, just making sure you know that you're phenomenal at everything you do. Being a mom, wife, cook, all that stuff," I cheesed and so did she.

"Aww, thank you, sweetie. I love you too," she neared me for a hug, and I squeezed her tightly before kissing her cheek.

I loved her so much, and I wanted her to know how great of a person she was, not just to her children but to my father as well. She did a lot for us, especially me because she got pregnant at seventeen. The fact that she was still able to get a Master's Degree without neglecting Kendrin or me, spoke volumes.

"See you later, Ma," I smirked.

"Bye son."

I left my parents' house so that I could get home to Gianna. As soon as I stepped foot in the door, I smelled food. I loved when my baby made Italian food because it was authentic. I swear I never wanted to eat at those fake ass Italian restaurants anymore, because it tasted like microwaved TV dinners now.

"Is that homemade pizza?" I questioned as I hugged her from behind.

"It's called Pizza pugliese," she corrected me and turned around to kiss my lips.

"Yeah, that," I smiled and she chuckled. "I love you Gianna, always and forever baby," I whispered and stared down into her eyes. I could feel her small belly poking me.

As I looked into her eyes, I thought about the things my father had just told me. I didn't ever want Gianna to leave me over some hoes, because it just wasn't worth it. She meant more to me than a half hour or more of pleasure.

"I love you too," she blushed.

"Where is your ring?" I looked at her hand.

"It's in my apron pocket. I took it off to cook," she said.

"Don't ever take that ring off," I stated sternly.

"Okay, sorry," she smacked her lips.

"I'm serious shorty, that ring means something," I sat down on the stool.

"I know Kendrick, which is why I took it off. I don't wanna lose it," she caressed my face and kissed me. "But now I'm done," she reached into her pocket and slid it back on.

"That's better," I bit my lip before tonguing her down.

I needed to keep myself in line, because I couldn't let these bitches cause me to lose my girl. And then with a baby on way, I really needed to shape up, because I wanted my family to be whole. How would my son feel knowing I didn't love or respect his mother enough to keep my dick in my pants? I know it wouldn't feel good, because it didn't feel good hearing my father tell me he cheated on my mother, and that was twenty plus years ago.

I WAS GOING over to my parents' house to chill with my little brothers, and just see how my parents were doing. Because I no longer
lived there with them, I wanted to make sure we stayed tight. I never
wanted it to be where I had no idea what was going on with my
family, especially my younger brothers.

I came inside the huge ass house, and went straight to the game
room where I found my little brothers Kendall and Kendlan playing
video games. I was definitely about to get in on that in a minute. The
system at this house was just as good as mine, maybe even better, so I
wanted to make sure I got to use it whenever I was over.

"Aye, where are mom and dad?" I asked, peeking my head into the
game room.

"Mom is the kitchen, and dad ain't here right now," Kendlan
replied, keeping his eyes on the game.

I walked to the kitchen and saw my mother making some tea.
"Guess who?" I covered her eyes from behind.

"Boy, you better move before I burn the both of us," she said and
chuckled.

"Dang Ma, why so violent?" I laughed. She turned around and I
hugged her tightly.

My mom was so pretty. She looked to be about thirty-one, even though she was knocking on forty's door soon. She was in great shape, had not a wrinkle in sight, and her hair hung down her small back.

"Sit down Kaleeini, I wanna talk to you," she said.

I frowned because it sounded like she had something serious to say. I sat down and stared into my mother's beautiful face, as I waited for her to speak on whatever was bothering her. She pushed her long hair behind her ears, and then sipped her tea.

"Someone robbed your brother... Kendall to be exact," she said and I shot up out of my seat. This was not some shit I expected to come out of her mouth. Niggas knew better than that.

"What?" I growled.

"Yeah, he was walking to his car, and someone robbed him at gunpoint. Now, I didn't tell your father because we don't need him coming out of retirement," she said.

"What the fuck!" I banged on the countertop and she cocked her head at me. "I mean what the crap, sorry Ma," I half smiled.

"Now, I'm only telling you because I wanted to see if you can find out who did it. I don't want you doing anything dumb, like trying to kill someone over this, Kaleeini. Maybe you could just keep a closer eye on your brother," she said.

"Yeah, okay Ma," I nodded. Fuck that, whoever robbed my brother better enjoy whatever he got, because that was a dead man walking. "I'm gonna go talk to Kendall," I said and kissed her cheek. She followed me out of the kitchen, and then she went upstairs as I headed to the game room. "Kendall, let me talk to you for a second," I said.

"Aight," he replied and paused the game. "I'm coming back, don't cheat nigga," he told Kendlan. I gripped the back of his neck and we walked to the den.

"Why you ain't tell me some niggas robbed you?" I frowned and folded my arms across my chest. We were standing across from one another in the narrow hallway that had brown laminate wall panels.

"Because man, how would that look?" He folded his arms as well.

"It ain't gon' look like nothing! You can't just let niggas get away with shit, Kendall!" I squinted my eyes.

What the fuck was he on? Wasn't nobody about to be robbing my family and getting away with that shit. I didn't care if it was my brother or my cousin twice removed, the perpetrator was getting blasted.

"When them niggas robbed me that was the first thing they said. 'I bet you gone tell your brother Kaleeini and cousin KJ'," he dropped his head. *Them niggas did that shit on purpose*, I thought.

See, that was the thing about being hood famous sometimes. People would do dumb shit just to say they violated you or your kin for bragging rights, or to get their name out there. Niggas was always tryna start small beefs with us or niggas we knew, just so they could say they had beef with a King. Only the niggas that we wouldn't allow to be down reacted in that way, because everyone else showed respect, hoping that one day they could get bread with us.

"And you should've said *you damn right nigga*," I told him.

"Leeini man, please do not handle this. I'm gon' look like a bitch," he pleaded with his words and his eyes.

"So, you just want me to allow these niggas to get away with robbing you? What they take?" I scowled. I understood his angle, but damn was it hard not to retaliate on his behalf.

"Just my iPod, my iPad, and my bracelet," he said like it was nothing.

"See, hell nah! I can't let these niggas punk my little brother!" I shouted.

"It ain't gon' happen again Kaleeini, just let this one go," he begged.

"What if dad finds out? You know it's gon' be a wrap, right? Won't be no begging and pleading, he gon' go after them niggas," I shook my head.

"I know and I'm hoping he won't find out," he looked me in the eyes, silently asking me to keep my mouth shut.

I really wanted to check these niggas for robbing my brother. I was gonna at least find out who the fuck they were, because this was unacceptable. I had no problem making examples out of niggas, as long as they wanted to keep disrespecting me. Something in my six-pack was telling me that this was not a simple bitch nigga wanting to rob a King, but so much more than that. I wasn't sure why I felt that way though.

I chopped it up with Kendall some more, and then waited for my dad to get home so I could see him as well. Kendall stayed near the whole time, making sure I didn't run my mouth. He didn't need to worry though, because the only way my dad would find out, would be after them niggas got murked. After my dad and I talked for a bit, I picked up some Chinese food for Aysia and I.

Lately she'd been obsessed with this greasy shit, especially the chicken egg rolls. I wanted to control her diet some more so she wouldn't develop heart disease or some shit, but my mom said to let her enjoy it, and buy her whatever meal she requested. She knew better than me so I was gonna listen. I ain't wanna argue over some damn Chinese food.

I walked into my home, and before I finished setting the food down, Aysia ran her pretty ass into the kitchen wearing a tube top and shorts. She had a slight bulge, but it wasn't to the point where she couldn't show her stomach. You would definitely do a double take, but it didn't look bad at all.

"Ooh, did you get me a soda too?" she beamed. I stared at her with my lips pursed and my arms folded. "Kaleeini, I can't eat this without my sodaaaa," she whined.

"Yeah man," I scoffed and got myself a bottle of water from the fridge.

"Thank you, baby," she tugged on my shirt, and I turned around to lean down and kiss her.

"Mmm, another," I said and she kissed me again.

"You gon' be fat even after the baby at this rate," I taunted.

"And you're still gonna love me," she raised a brow with her cocky ass.

"You right, I will. You lucky I love your little attitude, because otherwise we'd be a wrap if you blew up," I laughed and so did she.

"So you would love me even if I was five hundred pounds?" she grinned and hugged my torso.

"Damn, five hundred? I would try, but damn, babe. I'd have to get you some help," I cheesed and she burst into laughter.

"Good enough," she responded and bit her lip.

"Yeah, I'd butter those rolls for you," I joked and we laughed loudly in unison.

KJ and I were about to go eat breakfast since the snow was back to normal and not acting crazy. It was early January though, so it was still pretty nippy.

I reached into my cherry wood dresser for some tights, and when I tried to bring them around my waist, it squeezed my belly to death damn near. I had already grown out of my jeans, so tights were my last resort.

"What the fuck?" I said to myself. I was trying to think if I washed them wrong, making them shrink. I tried to adjust them again, but they were not even close to being able to make it around my bottom half without strangling my waistline. KJ walked his fine ass into the bedroom, saw what I was doing, and then laughed. "I think I washed these wrong," I shook my head and slid them down.

"I think it's from those liquor store honey buns shorty," he laughed.

"Huh?" I frowned.

"You eat three of them every day, and the baby has grown a lot too," he stared at me.

I walked to the mirror and lifted my shirt, to see I was definitely way bigger than before. I guess because I'd been rocking nightgowns and KJ's t-shirts, I hadn't noticed too much. I rubbed my round stomach as KJ chuckled at me.

"It's cool baby, you get a pass for your behavior," he said making me smile. "My son likes honey buns... my nigga," he joked and we chuckled.

"Whatever," I waved him off as I fished in my drawer for some sweats.

They fit perfectly on my waist, when before they were a little baggy, so I knew what KJ said was true.

We headed to Miss Shirley's Cafe, because we both wanted her coconut cream French toast. As soon as my butt hit the seat, I was ready to order my food, so the waiter took our orders right away.

Right when she left, some hoe walked by eyeing KJ like he was on the menu, and his ass was smiling back like he was ready to go in her fucking oven.

"Good morning," she smiled seductively.

"Morning, shorty," KJ responded nonchalantly, but I still didn't like it.

This girl was beautiful as hell. She appeared to be about 5'7, had a big round ass, small waist, and perfect D cups with plenty of cleavage. Her perfume smelled expensive, and her weave was fresh and perfectly wand curled. She had on a tan wrap dress that hugged every curve on her body, while I was sitting here in sweats, a t-shirt, UGGs, and a pullover. My hair was hanging down messily, and I wore no makeup or earrings. I pulled my Chapstick from my purse to give me some sort of damn appeal.

"You are so disrespectful," I folded my arms and shook my head.

"What did I do, shorty?" he asked dryly as if I was overreacting.

"You're smiling at that bitch like I'm not sitting right fucking here!" I was so fucking angry it was crazy. I hated that she looked better than me right now. I knew I should've worn a dress too.

"Oh my gosh Gigi, I can't smile at people?" he frowned. I couldn't even talk. I just shook my head as a tear ran down my cheek. "Shorty don't cry-" he stopped talking and got up to sit next to me. "Gianna, what are you crying for?" He kissed my face, and moved my hair out the way.

"Because you're so stupid and you don't get it," I wiped my face with my fingertips.

"Baby, I just smiled at her because she smiled at me and that is it, I swear to you. I wasn't smiling because I liked her or anything Gigi. Relax shorty," he picked my face up and kissed me gently.

"I saw you oogling her breasts, KJ," I turned my lip up.

"What? No I wasn't. You know I prefer them smaller," he squeezed one of mine while grinning. I knew his ass was lying but I didn't care; it still felt good to hear. "I wouldn't trade this sexy little body, that pretty face, that phenomenal pussy, or the baby you're carrying for no hoe. I love you and only you, aight?" He raised his brows and I nodded before smiling. "You're a fucking brat, man," he chuckled and got up to go sit back across from me as I giggled.

The rest of the breakfast date went well, and KJ made sure not to look at anybody that walked by the table unless it was the waiter. A couple more thirsties sauntered by staring him down, but he paid them no mind just like I wanted. As soon as I dropped this baby I was gonna be checking bitches left and right again. Afterward we went to Starbucks for hot chocolate, and then went home.

"Do you want the rest of yours?" I questioned as we walked into our home.

"Damn you finished already?" He asked and I nodded my head while laughing. "Here," he handed me the rest of his drink and then closed the door behind me.

We walked through the large spacious foyer, until we made it to the den area and he took my jacket off my shoulders.

"What are you gonna do about pants shorty?" he quizzed as we sat down on the couch. He reached down to remove my UGGs for me, and then placed my feet in his lap to massage them.

"I have to buy maternity ones I guess," I shrugged and sipped his hot chocolate.

"What is that?" he furrowed his brows.

"They have a stretchy waistline so the baby won't get squished," I snickered.

"You get that, because if you squash my baby I'm gon' have to hurt you," he smirked.

"I may like that," I raised a brow.

"Oh yeah," he responded and tugged down my sweats. I finished off the hot chocolate by tipping it back, and then set it on the glass end table. He pulled me closer to him, lifted my shirt off of my body, and unhooked my bra. "I am loving these," he said as he cupped my now C cups.

Told you his ass was lying. He better not get used to these, because my mom said I'd be right back to being a member of the itty bitty titty committee, soon after the baby arrived. I was bummed to hear that but oh well.

I reached under his thermal, moved it upward so I could get it off, and then wrapped my arms around his neck for a kiss.

"Lift up," he whispered and I did so. He unbuckled his pants, and then I got off to let him get out of them. Once he was naked and looking good enough to eat, he sat back down so that I could straddle him. As soon as his tip entered me, a loud moan burst through my lips. It hurt so good. "Oh my gosh," he grunted as his hands roamed my body and squeezed my breasts. "I love pregnant pussy. This shit stays wet as fuck."

"Uuhh, aaah," I whimpered as he spread my legs some more, and moved me up and down on his pole.

"Keep doing that, Gianna," he bit his lip as he stared down into his lap to see what was going on.

"Aahhh," I cooed as I released for the first time on him. He hugged me against his body, and then squeezed my ass roughly while spreading my cheeks. "Kendrick, aaahh, uuhh," I called out as he kissed on my neck and bit my shoulders.

"Get on your back," he demanded.

I climbed off of him and laid on my back like he'd asked. He got on top of me, entered me, and then proceeded to go ham. "Aaah, uuhh, aaahh, uuuh," I yelled as he hit my spot with intensity.

"Oh shit, fuck," he moaned as he sucked on my lips. I gushed on him as he beat my center to a pulp, and soon after, he exploded. "Shit!" he called out after making his orgasm sound.

I loved the moan that came from his mouth when he reached his peak. It was like a soft, breathy grunt. I grabbed his face, and we let our tongues dance for a little bit. He then got up, put me on all fours, and slipped into me from behind. He was never done after his first nut. He put one of my arms behind my back, and then craned his neck around to suck my nipple while plunging into me from behind.

———

Because of schedule conflicts, I hadn't seen my friends all at once since I'd been back. I couldn't wait to get them all together, because I was going crazy with this information on London. I knew their minds were gonna be blown just like mine; no pun intended.

"Okay baby, I'll be back around 8," Kendrick peeked his head into my relaxation room.

"Alright, bye," I said, and Willow, Aysia, and Shannon waved to him as well. As soon as I heard the security system ding, I knew he was gone. "Alright, so, me and KJ were at the cabin chilling and getting cozy-"

"Ooooh," Willow cheesed.

"Calm down, hoe," I put my hand up and we all laughed. "Anyway, so he and I are kissing and exchanging I love you's, when suddenly the living room light comes on. Why when we looked to see who it was, it was that old bitch that he used to fuck!" I squealed and they bucked their eyes.

"Wait, she traveled all the way up there?" Aysia frowned. "For what?"

"For some dick I guess, but let me finish telling you. So she's crying hysterically about how much she loves KJ, and then of course he dissed her. She then pulls a gun from her jacket, and blows her own head open," I finished and they stared at me in disbelief.

"She killed herself? Over KJ?" Shannon quizzed and I nodded slowly with my eyes closed.

"Are you sure she was just a fuck buddy?" Willow raised her brow. "Because if I'm willing to take my life, it ain't gon' be over no once in a while dick that I can't even call my own."

"I know, that's what I was thinking, but KJ assured me she was just crazy. And plus, remember when she tried to press he and I at the club? She seemed a little off then," I reminded them.

"Oh, you mean when he spent one hundred years in the bathroom with her? And then barked for you to leave them be?" Shannon cocked her head.

"Yeah, but he was just straightening her out," I said, even though I was starting to doubt myself.

"Or maybe he was telling her something that he tells you too," Shannon countered. I knew because of her situation with Kenzie that she was weary of everyone, but I refused to believe KJ would do that to me.

"I don't think so. KJ loves me and I just know he wouldn't do that," I shrugged.

"Yeah, and Mrs. King hates that old bitch, so I doubt KJ would be trying to have anything serious with her," Willow said and Aysia nodded in agreement.

"I just can't believe the bitch killed herself over young ass KJ!" Aysia laughed.

"This is Willow Jameson reporting live from WBAL-TV here in Baltimore, and Ms. Daniels we have to know, is the dick that good?" Willow placed her fist to my mouth as if it were a microphone, as we all laughed at her crazy ass.

"Well, Ms. Jameson, I must confirm that the dick may just be that good. I've become a better person now that I've experienced a dick of that caliber," I responded as they cracked up.

I was convinced that KJ was being honest with me, and that London was just out of her mind. I mean KJ was addictive, and I guess she saw what I saw in him, and fell in love just like I did. Lucky for me, he loved me back.

Gianna and I were out shopping for some maternity wear, specifically jeans. I didn't need it just yet, but I wanted to be prepared unlike her ass. She had grown out of her jeans a while back, but now she couldn't fit into her tights anymore, so it was a must we got her some pants.

"You like these?" I lifted a pair in the air and she turned her nose up. They weren't that cute, but they would do for me.

"What happened to your shoes Aysia?" Gianna asked me and frowned down.

"Oh, just got some coffee on them," I shrugged.

They did look pretty bad, but I wanted to keep them on in case I ran into any more mishaps. No point in ruining a perfectly new pair, when I could just run these already damaged ones into the ground.

"You can't clean them?" she questioned.

"I'm sure I can but I didn't feel like it. Kaleeini bought me some more but I don't wanna wear them yet," I explained and she nodded.

We picked out some jeans and dresses, and then took them to the counter to pay. As we were walking out of the store, some chick bumped me hard as fuck, to the point where I swear I felt my little baby move up and down.

"Oh, my bad," she looked over her shoulder at me and smirked.

"What the fuck? All this damn space to walk and she has to squeeze by me?" I rolled my eyes.

I swear people had been getting on my fucking nerves with the rudeness lately! They needed to take their asses to New York with that bullshit!

"She's lucky we're both pregnant, or she might have gotten that ass beat," Gianna responded and I nodded in agreement.

God was looking out for her, because with the way I was feeling right now, if I didn't have something more important growing in my body, my foot would've been deep off in her ass by now. Bitch bumped me so hard my shoulder was throbbing. I knew she did that shit on purpose, but like I said, I couldn't sweat it too much for health reasons.

We went to another store just to look around, and in walked that same girl who bumped into me. I paid her no mind, and continued sifting through the clothes. She started shopping my same rack, and stepped on the back of my UGG. They may have been in pretty bad shape already, but it still pissed me the fuck off.

"Look bitch, I don't know what your problem is but you got me fucked up," I turned around to face her. She had that same smug look on her face from earlier.

"It was an accident boo, quit tripping," she grinned just as Gianna came to stand by me.

"What's the problem?" Gianna asked like her pregnant ass could do anything. She was further along than me yet trying to tussle.

"Didn't you date Brice?" she cocked her head and squinted her eyes as if she wasn't too sure.

I could tell by the smile hiding somewhere in her expression, that she already knew the answer to that. I'll be damned if I'm dealing with Brice's groupies while I'm in a whole new relationship.

"Why?" I frowned.

"You set him up. I know you had your new man take care of him.

You one of them sneaky bitches," she smacked her lips and shook her head as she looked me up and down.

"Ain't nobody set that nigga up, so you can quit with the ugly faces," Gianna spat and I put my arm in front of her feisty ass.

"Who the fuck are you? One of his hoes?" I folded my arms after making sure Gianna wasn't gonna move.

"Nah, I'm his home girl. But you better watch your back because the streets don't like bitches like you, *Aysia*," she gritted and then switched her ass towards the exit of the store. "And when they get your ass, I'll be happy to take care of that fine ass King you got on your hands," she laughed referring to Kaleeini, and then walked out.

I watched her leave as my heart began to beat fast. This is exactly why I didn't want shit to get started between Kaleeini and Brice. I don't know what Kaleeini did with Brice, but I knew it was something, and now my name was tarnished. You did not wanna be known as a snitch in these streets, whether you were a girl or a guy. Niggas who didn't even know you would kill you just because you're a snitch. They didn't want you walking the Earth if they knew you ran your mouth.

"What the hell is her problem?" Gianna scowled.

"I don't know, but I'm sure a couple other people have the same fucking problem with me that she has," I shook my head still staring at the exit, even though that bitch had long disappeared. I didn't even wanna be in public right now with the way I was feeling.

After the mall, I took Gianna home, and then went to my house that I shared with Kaleeini. I didn't want to mention today to him, because he was adamant that whoever threw coffee on me had robbed his little brother as well. However, I learned my lesson about not telling him shit, and I wasn't gonna do that again. Who knows, me keeping this information could have me lying dead somewhere. Telling Kaleeini could possibly save my life, and remove the rat moniker from being attached to my name.

I found him in the bedroom, sleep on the couch we had in there. I laughed because he chose to sleep on that instead of the bed. I sat on the edge by his chest, and caressed his sexy face. I moved his dreads out of the way, and kissed his cheek. He hopped up, and then calmed down when he saw it was me.

"Sorry baby, a nigga was having a nightmare," he exhaled and dropped his face into his hands. His dreads fell forward as he wiped his eyes.

"Because you need to stop watching *American Horror Story* every night," I grinned.

"Maybe you're right," he sat up and cackled. I turned him to face me, and planted a nice wet kiss on his lips.

"Did you get enough stuff?" he inquired and I nodded.

"Yeah. Kaleeini, today some girl approached me and said that I needed to watch my back since I set Brice up," I just got straight to the point. He looked at me and laughed, which was not the reaction I expected. I needed him to take this seriously because I was scared. "What's so funny?"

"That is, they not about to do shit. And what kind of niggas send a bitch to approach you? Matter fact, why are they approaching you at all? They need to get at the niggas that actually did something to Brice," he stood up and removed his shirt.

"I know but I'm scared a little," I admitted. I was really fearful now that I saw Kaleeini thought this was a joke.

"Scared of what, baby? I would never let anything happen to you, especially while pregnant. Do not worry, you don't need to watch your back because I got it," he smiled and that in turn made me smile.

"You always know what to say to make me feel better," I hugged his torso since he was too tall for me to hug his neck.

"That's my job," he pulled away and then bent my head back to kiss me passionately.

I was at the gym with my little sister Kendria, hoping to get a good workout in. I don't know why her ass insisted on coming, knowing that she wasn't gonna be doing shit but walking slow as hell on the treadmill, and texting on her phone. She just liked to get out in hopes of seeing some shit that she could run back and tell our girl cousins. If you wanted everyone to know something, tell my baby sister.

I looked to my right at her, and her little ass was reading a text and walking on the treadmill like she had molasses in her ass.

"Why the fuck you even come, Dria?" I frowned.

"Because I need to keep my body together," she smacked her lips. I swear she was my mom's twin. They were both naturally slim thick, and it didn't take much for them to stay that way.

"Who the fuck you keeping your body together for? And what you weigh? One hundred pounds even?" I taunted.

"I weigh one hundred and ten, you asshole, and I'm keeping my body together for myself thank you," she rolled her eyes. "I ain't looking to impress no niggas," she said.

"You better not be. Not unless they're ready to go against Dad, and every other King man in the family," I replied.

"How am I gonna get married one day? Daddy said I can't date until I'm twenty-seven," she frowned and looked over at me.

"That's a good age, Dria," I smiled, feeling kind of bad for her and any nigga that wanted her.

I couldn't imagine ever being okay knowing some nigga was sticking his dick in my little sister. If my Dad, KJ, Kendrae, and I could have it our way, she would be a nun.

"Nope, when I turn eighteen, I'm gon' have me a man. He's gon' be a big buff thug so that he can whoop you, KJ, and Kendrae's ass if I need him to," she said and burst into laughter.

"Good luck finding that bitch ass nigga," I scoffed and chuckled even though I didn't want to.

I ain't never lost a fight in my life, and I've been in more than I can count. If a nigga is ever able to whoop my ass, I'm gon' fight his ass every time I see him until I win or he kills my ass.

"Thank you, because I will."

"Whatever. Put your fucking phone down so we can really work-out," I told her.

"I'm having an important conversation right now, Kendrin," she bucked her eyes and continued reading.

"You don't talk to nobody but Kaylie and Kendlie," I snatched her phone and put it in the cup holder of my machine. I low key checked to make sure she wasn't texting some nigga though.

"You're so annoying!" she grunted and started running on the belt like she was some pro athlete.

"Don't kill yourself, shorty," I laughed at her as I started running on the treadmill as well.

After about an hour of me running, and Kendria walking and talking my ear off about all kinds of shit, we headed upstairs to the weight room. Kendria sat on the abs machine, and wanted me to stand there to monitor her.

As I was watching my sister to make sure she was doing it right, I saw a familiar face out the corner of my eye. I sipped my Gatorade, and discreetly looked over to see who it was. It was Rosalind kissing on some random nigga. *Already?* I thought.

"You weren't even watching!" Kendria snapped me from my thoughts.

"Yes I was, do ten more," I turned my lip and then looked back over at Rosalind with her new nigga.

They started coming this way holding hands, just as Kendria stood up. Rosalind didn't even notice us as she walked by, because she was so enthralled like she was in love or some shit. I didn't want her to see me though, so I was good with that.

"Ain't that old girl?" Kendria said loudly as fuck. I could smack her ass. Rosalind looked over at us, and I could tell she was nervous as fuck. "What's your name again?" Kendria asked before Rosalind could keep walking away, and her man looked confused.

"Rosalind," she responded and glanced at me nervously before putting her attention back on Kendria.

"Right," Kendria nodded as I paid them no mind.

"This your new man?" Kendria's nosey ass looked him up and down.

"New? I wouldn't say I was new. It's been six months," he responded surprising the fuck out of both of us. This bitch was a for real skeezer yo.

"Well nice seeing y'all, come on baby," Rosalind pulled old boy by the hand.

Kendria turned to me with her jaw damn near on the floor like mine. "Did he say six months?" She bucked her eyes.

"How the fuck do you even know her?" I frowned.

"She followed me on Instagram and I think she forgot to unfollow me. So I was snooping through her page and found Brooke, and I just put two and two together," she shrugged. "But I heard Aunt Jessica telling mom about Kenzie getting her pregnant," she nodded with a smile and I shook my head.

"She followed you?" I furrowed my brows. That must've been how she found out my name wasn't David. Scheming ass hoe.

"Yeah, it was a while ago, but occasionally I check to see who unfollowed me so I can unfollow their asses back, and she was in the list of people that followed me but *I* didn't follow back, so I clicked to see who she was," Kendria folded her arms.

"Damn, women are fucking detectives," I shook my head. "I think that was her real baby daddy," I added.

"Oh shit! That's some tea if so!" Kendria laughed and clapped her hands. "I heard Aunt Jessica say Kenzie was confused because he strapped up. I tried to text Shannon for more scoop but she wasn't texting back."

"Tea? What the fuck are you talking about?" I frowned. "And what you know about niggas strapping up and shit," I seethed.

"Tea, like gossip," she explained. "And I know plenty of things, Kendrin. Just because I'm a virgin don't mean I'm ignorant to certain things," she turned her nose up.

"Do not say nothing to Shannon about seeing this hoe with another nigga, until I tell Kenzie first. He needs to be the one to look into this," I told her.

"What makes you think I was gonna tell Shannon?" she grinned.

"Because you can't hold water, Kendria," I laughed and so did she.

"If you tell me not to tell, I won't. But if you don't give me that disclaimer, I'm gon' tell," she placed her hand on her small hip.

Some big ass jailbird looking nigga walked by and licked his lips at her. He then looked at me, and we glared at each other as he kept walking. This nigga had to be a fucking champion body builder.

"Bring yo' ass on. Got these old ass buff niggas looking at you," I took her hand into mine.

"Who?" she flung her hair, trying to look around as I pulled her. "That's the type I'm looking for!"

"That big burly nigga. If he wasn't so fucking huge I would've checked his ass," I said and we both burst into laughter as we exited. I may be an undefeated fighter, but I would definitely need some heat to go against that nigga.

TWO DAYS LATER...

I PULLED up to Kendrin's house because he said he wanted to talk to me about some shit. I wasn't really in the mood, because Shannon was still tripping on me. She acted as if all was good that day in the school parking lot, but she was right back to ignoring me the next damn day. I was starting to feel defeated, and a part of me wanted to give up, but I loved her. I knew I wouldn't be okay if she moved on and got with another nigga. I also knew that I wouldn't be able to be with another girl for a long while. And even if I got a girl, Shannon would always have my heart. I would end up in another love triangle and I was not interested in that shit in any way, shape, or form.

Once Kendrin's gates opened, I drove through and parked anywhere. Since he had to let me through the gates, he knew I was here and was standing in his doorway already.

"What's up?" I slapped hands with him and hugged him once I neared his door.

"Shit, a lot," he shook his head as I hit the alarm on my car, and walked through the door into his foyer.

Willow walked past me and gave me a half hug. I could see in her face that she had some anger towards me, and I really couldn't blame her. That was her friend and I did her dirty, what could I say?

I followed Kendrin to his arcade like room that had expensive leather couches, and all kinds of games that you usually see at Chuck E. Cheese or some shit. It just made me think about how I wanted my own place, so that I could fix that shit up how I wanted. I sat down and he handed me a can of soda, which I immediately opened.

"So what do you have to tell me? I'm anxious as hell," I said as I leaned against the back of the couch.

"Alright, so two days ago, Kendria and I were at the gym and we saw Rosalind there," he said and looked into my eyes.

"Alright," I responded and took another sip of my soda.

"And she was with this guy and they were pretty cozy; you know, kissing and shit," he continued.

Although I didn't *love* Rosalind, I still had feelings for her because she was my girl at one point, and for a long ass time. Hearing that she was already on to the next one had me feeling some type of way; especially since she'd just lost our fucking baby. I was starting to see that she was a hoe for sure.

"Anyway, Kendria's nosey ass asked her about him, and he said that he and Rosalind have been together since six months ago," he finished and I swallowed the lump in my throat.

This bitch Rosalind had more secrets than a muthafucka. It seemed like lately she was always dropping bombs on me. I really had no idea who this hoe was, and I can't believe I felt bad for fucking around on her. And to think I may have possibly lost the girl I loved, all because I wanted to protect her fucking loose pussy ass feelings. I was holding my can of soda so tight that I was waiting for it to explode in my hands.

"He said six months, huh?" I sipped my soda calmly despite my thoughts, and Kendrin nodded wearing a sympathetic expression. I stared off into space and thought about how bad my hand was itching to go across that bitch's face. I didn't care that I had basically done the same thing to her. I'm just being fucking honest.

"I was just as surprised as you. I mean, not only has she been with him, but she gave me the pussy pretty easily too," he reminded me, causing my jaw to tighten.

"Yeah, I know," I dropped my head and then picked it back up to finish the soda. I could only imagine if I had actually been faithful to this girl. I would've been crushed, and she would've had twenty bullets in her body.

"I don't think that was your baby either. I mean you strapped up, so did I, and he probably didn't," he said. I felt like Kendrin was squeezing a lemon over the wounds I'd just suffered from, and I didn't wanna hear anymore.

"Well, thanks for the info," I smiled. I stood up and we dapped each other up again.

"You good?" he quizzed.

"Yeah man, I'm straight. A hoe gon' be a hoe, right?" I grinned and so did he.

"I know that's right," he exhaled and chuckled.

I left out of his house, and sat in my car for a little bit. I didn't know if I was angry because my ego was bruised, or because I actually cared for Rosalind a little. I mean, who was she? She had another boyfriend *and* she let my cousin hit. At least with me I only had Shannon. I didn't have a million other bitches too! I can't believe I jeopardized my relationship over that fucking hoe.

Who am I kidding though, neither one of us were in the right. However, I was interested to know about this fucking baby. Kendrin had a point about me strapping up with her every time.

I pulled my phone out and cued up Rosalind's phone number. I was about to press it, until I decided to just pop up. I wanted to possibly run into her while chilling with this nigga, and if she knew I was coming she may send him off somewhere. I wanted to see if he knew what kind of girl Rosalind was. If he knew she was my bitch and still chose to fuck with her anyway, I may knock his ass out.

I put my phone down and sped out of Kendrin's driveway until I made it to Rosalind's little apartment building in Coppin Heights. I couldn't get out of the car fast enough, and I ran to her door to damn near beat it down. A few moments later, a nigga answered and I was happy my plan worked.

"Can I help you?" he frowned.

"Yeah, is Rosalind in?" I folded my arms.

He was average height I guess; about 5'10, brown skinned, and had dreads. He looked real frumpy, and it made me wonder why she would choose to fuck around with this nigga. I mean at least Shannon was bad as fuck, and way better looking than her.

"Yes, can I ask what you want with her?" he frowned up at me.

"I wanted to check on her you know, since she miscarried our *child*," I smiled and put an emphasis on the word child.

"Nigga, what the fuck is you talking about?" he barked. Rosalind finally came to the door, and her eyes almost popped out her head.

"Oh wait, you thought you were the dad?" I furrowed my brows.

"I *was* the dad, I had a test ran nigga. Now what the fuck are you talking about?" he growled.

"I'm talking about you been fucking my bitch for the last six months!" I hollered and brushed past him into the house.

"Your bitch? Rosalind, what the fuck is this dude talking about?" he glared at her. Where was he the past six months, because I'm surprised we never crossed paths. I had never seen this guy before.

"Umm Pablo, see I-"

"And where the fuck you been hiding him I ain't never seen this nigga in my life!" I hissed.

"He went to jail three months after we got together, but he got me pregnant before he left obviously," she explained nervously.

That shit ain't sound right, but I didn't know what to believe right now. My brain was overheating, and I didn't have the right mindset to sit down and calculate.

"Yet you tried to pin the baby on me," I nodded and laughed angrily.

"Aye, ain't you Kenzie King? You on the starting five for Morgan State," he squinted his eyes.

"Nice to me meet you bruh," I said sarcastically. "What the fuck did you mess up my relationship for when you had a nigga!" I barked.

"Because regardless you still cheated on me!" Rosalind screamed, and tears flowed down her cheeks. I could see in her eyes that her heart was still broken because of me. But why if she had someone?

"Rosalind, you got me fucked up!" this cat Pablo yelled at her.

"And after your little bitch killed my baby you shouldn't have shit to say to me if it's not an apology!" she cried harder, ignoring Pablo.

"I been apologized, countless times," I scoffed.

Pablo snapped his neck to look at me, and I could tell he blamed me for Shannon's mistake.

"I'm gone," I chucked the deuces up and walked out.

Any dealings I had with Rosalind were a wrap. I'm just mad I got caught up with such a grimy ass little bitch!

As soon as that nigga Kenzie left, I slammed the door behind him angrily. I peeked out of Rosalind's window, and waited until I saw him pull off in his truck. Once he was gone, I turned to look at her with a smile.

"I don't know about this Pab," she held her biceps as if she was cold.

"What the fuck you don't know? Just follow with the plan, and I promise you gon' be good," I frowned and plopped down on the couch.

That whole little fiasco that just took place was all a part of the plan, in a way. I was just over here to visit Rosalind to discuss some things, but when he happened to pop up, we decided to give him the show. However, the whole gym thing was definitely planned out from beginning to end. I didn't know Rosalind from a can of paint, but I did fuck one time. That baby was definitely not mine, but we were gonna pretend like it was. It was gonna be my way of getting these niggas' attention.

See, I'd been trying to get at these King niggas for the longest, but

I couldn't touch them or anything they did. I needed to stir up some kind of noise, so that I could get my name out there. I wanted to take these niggas out, but I needed the streets to know there was a beef in order to toughen up my character. Not only did I want to take over the drug game, but I wanted that fame them niggas had. See, there was no better way to get your name popping like some beef. And this wouldn't be beef with some regular Joe Blow ass niggas, these mutha-fuckin' King niggas were crime royalty, coincidentally.

Was I scared that they would kill my ass? Hell no, because I knew how to hide out and snake through shit. I wanted them to get word that I didn't fuck with them, and then my name would start to pass through town. I would be able to recruit niggas and get connects based of my so-called beef, because it would make me appear to be more established in the game than I am. It's almost like when people will try and start something with a celebrity that's more famous than them, just so people will start checking for them too. I was finna come up off these niggas in the easiest way.

Niggas only made enemies with niggas that were their equal, and that's exactly what people would see me as if this worked out correctly. And shit, if they did catch me and kill me, I would still go out more well-known than I am now.

I met Rosalind six months ago, and I was just looking to smash. We ended up getting high and shit, and she blabbed to me that she was the girlfriend of Kenzie King. A light bulb went off in my head immediately, and I planned to start this shit then. Unfortunately, I actually did get locked up for some petty robberies and shit, so I wasn't able to do what I needed to do. By the time I got out, which was a month ago, Rosalind hated Kenzie and agreed to my plan of taking his family out before I even finished running down the details. I guess going to jail helped me in the end, because before I went she had her head so far up his ass it was ridiculous.

"I don't understand, Pablo, I'm not trying to die!" Rosalind yelled snapping me from my thoughts.

"Shorty you're not gonna fucking die. Look all you're doing is helping my name start to ring bells. Once I become known as the rival of the Kings, muthafuckas will start to fall in line," I rubbed her smooth thigh. "Once they do, I will break you off some bread and let you go on about your way."

All the niggas that couldn't be down with the Kings would be running to me for the chance to go against these niggas while making money. The Kings thought they were so much better than everybody, and damn near screened everyone before letting them get down. I was gonna scrape up all them niggas that they denied entry to, and form a solid ass team. I was gonna gain control, all off the coat tails of the King men. They would build my name for me through this beef, while I sat back and did nothing but formed the strongest army I could against them. Unlike their enemies in the past, I was gonna wait until I was well prepared to fuck shit up. Wasn't gonna be no premature ejaculation over this way.

So why didn't I just join them? The answer was simple; they wouldn't let me. About ten months before I went to jail, I attempted to try and work for them. I was broke and desperate, so I was willing to take on anything. They told me I wasn't fit, and that they weren't looking for any new people. What the fuck kind of shit is that? This ain't no damn department store, how you just tell someone you ain't looking for new people? So you see, I had to take them out in order to live, man. They had everything on lock so I couldn't even build my own empire from the ground up or anything.

Hit me up when a gun click don't make you flinch, I thought back to the last words that bitch nigga KJ said to me before dismissing me. He had his homie Lenny put a gun in my face, and when he pulled the trigger I jumped and pissed on myself. They laughed their asses off, and then let me know the gun was empty. Just thinking about it had my heart beating fast.

"Did you see Kenzie's face when you said it was your baby? Can I tell him the truth once you take over?" she questioned.

"If he's alive," I chuckled and pulled a blunt from my pocket. "But are you even sure he's the father?" I asked and lit the tip.

"No, it belonged to this guy I met when I went to this weekend function in D.C., but it was Kenzie's 'cause I said it was," she glared at me. This bitch was a for real hoe man.

"Aight, excuse me," I chuckled and took a pull.

" I should've never let you say it was yours, because now he's never gonna believe me down the line," she sighed and dropped her face into her hands. "And do you really have to kill Kenzie?" she frowned. "What if you just kill everyone else?" she smiled.

"If you love this nigga so, how was I and all these other niggas able to fuck?" I inquired. I just had to know, because she was busting it open for everybody. I'd even heard that she fucked Kenzie's cousin.

"Look, people make mistakes, just try not to hurt Kenzie. But that girl of his, can we kidnap and rape her or something?" she grinned.

"Just because it's you, I will see what I can do," I smiled and so did she.

Rosalind was cool as fuck and I had no problem helping her. I would gladly rough Kenzie's bitch up, and if she was fine I had no qualms about sticking my dick in her.

ONE MONTH LATER...

TODAY I WAS MEETING with a caterer so that I could taste his food for the wedding. He was supposedly the best in not just Baltimore, but all of Maryland. I was hoping he was, because his price quotes were sky high.

Gianna, Shannon, and Aysia agreed to come along, since Kendrin claimed he didn't care what kind of food was at the wedding, as long as we had some wings. His mother Nic, and my mother Cassandra, also decided to come along, and I was happy because I really wanted some help from them.

My mom had never been married to my father since he was killed in the army, but she was really organized and always planned well, so that would come in handy. Mrs. King, or Nic as she wanted us to call her, had been married for twenty years. She actually had two weddings she said, so I really wanted her input too.

We entered the empty restaurant since Kendrin paid for a private tasting, and a hostess seated the six of us at a table. I was starved and so ready to throw down, so I hoped this nigga didn't keep us waiting.

"So Aysia and Gianna, how are you guys feeling?" Nic asked.

"I'm doing okay, I'm just not used to always being so hungry, especially for sweet stuff," Aysia responded.

"Yeah, me too. I used to work out three times a week, but now I just wanna eat honey buns, pickles, and lasagna, while I watch TV," Gianna added and everyone laughed.

"Oh yes, I remember those days. But the good part is that no one can say anything to you because of the baby," my mother said and Nic nodded.

"I know I hated mushrooms, but when I got pregnant with my first baby I loved them. I used to have Kendrick buy me the huge jars of them, and sometimes I would eat them as they were, or put them over my food," Nic chuckled and so did we.

"KJ hates mushrooms!" Gianna laughed.

"That's probably why, because I used to eat them all the time," Nic smiled.

"Hello ladies, which one of you is Ms. Jameson?" The chef came out to our table, and looked around at all of us.

"That's me," I responded.

"Great, nice to meet you. I'm Chef La'Touche, and I'm gonna be the one preparing the dishes for today," he explained.

"Oh okay, well I can't wait," I cheesed and rubbed my palms together.

"Great. Is everybody ready to eat?" He asked the table and we all simultaneously nodded with smiles. We chatted for a little longer, and finally some waitresses started bringing out plates. "Okay so this would be the appetizer here. It's the bruschetta with leeks, goat cheese, which is just feta so don't freak out," he chuckled and so did we. "And it also has bacon on it," he announced the dish as the waiters set it in front of us.

"I like this!" Shannon beamed. I wanted to pick it just because I hadn't seen a smile on her face in forever, and if this could do that it was a winner.

"Yeah me too," my mother nodded her head.

"Here is the other choice. It's a chicken salad with walnuts, watermelon pick de gallo, honey chicken breast, blue cheese, and grape tomatoes," he explained as they brought the salad out.

"I love this one," Nic said as she ate it.

"Yeah it's so good," Gianna agreed.

"I think this one is better," Shannon added and Aysia agreed.

"Mom?" I looked down the table at her.

"Oh girl, I was too busy tearing it up," she said and everyone chuckled. "But yes this is the winner," she pointed to it with her fork before continuing to eat.

We went on to taste the main course, desserts, virgin and non-virgin cocktails as well. Unfortunately, Nic and my mom were the only ones who got to taste the non-virgin ones. At the end, I decided on the salad and the bacon wrapped scallops with chili butter for the appetizer, spicy barbecue wings like Kendrin wanted, and chicken mozzarella pasta for the main course with some sides. Then I chose blackberry cheesecake for dessert, which Gianna was happy about. Nic suggested having an open bar so that people could choose in case they didn't like the drinks I chose, and I agreed.

Nic and my mother hugged and kissed us goodbye, and we stayed behind to talk a little bit, just because we didn't feel comfortable talking about some things in front of the mothers.

"So Shannon, I haven't seen you smile like that in a while," Aysia said.

"I know, it felt good to think about something other than Kenzie," she sighed.

"So you're still mad? Or what's going through your head?" Gianna inquired.

"I'm angry at him, and I'm angry at myself for wanting to be with him still," she ran her hands over her face.

"I guess it's gonna take time to get over him," I said.

"But do you wanna move on? Or you just want space?" Aysia asked just as Shannon's phone lit up. Kenzie had been calling her during the tasting, but she had it on silent so it wouldn't disturb us.

"I don't know. Some days I want just a little space, and some days I'm so mad I never want to see him again," she replied.

I could tell she was really conflicted, but I didn't want to tell her what to decide. My friends and I never did stuff like that. We'd suggest but never tell you what to do.

"Just give it time, I'm sure you will come to some sort of conclusion," I said.

"It doesn't help that he blows you up though, huh?" Gianna sipped her water and Shannon shook her head no before dropping it.

ALTHOUGH A MONTH HAD GONE BY, Kenzie hadn't slowed up with his efforts to get me back. He called me all the time, texted me, sent me flowers, gifts, and everything. He was wearing me down like crazy, and I didn't want him to. I was waiting for the moment that I woke up and finally didn't care about him anymore, but that time had yet to come. I was still just as much in love with him as before. I think it may have been worse because now I was yearning for his touch and his presence. I missed his smile, his jokes, and the talks we used to have about our future. I wanted my nigga back so bad but I knew I just couldn't give in.

For the past month he'd been saying he wanted to talk to me about something, but I never responded. Today, I finally agreed because I just needed a hug from him to keep me going. He was like a drug to me at this point. Like I said, I wasn't getting any better as time passed like I thought I would.

I was leaving class with Kenzie heavy on my mind, and accidentally bumped someone.

"Oh shoot, I'm sorry," I turned to apologize. It was a guy who was about 6 feet even, light skinned, deep brown eyes, and perfect features. *Damn*, I thought. I think he was in my class, but I wasn't sure because that class was my biggest one.

"Oh, no worries. Christian," he stuck his hand out to me.

"Shannon. Again, I'm sorry about bumping into you," I blushed.

"Nah, you're good shorty. As beautiful as you are I would let you bump me like that any day," he flirted, making me push my hair behind my ears. "You have a man or anything? I wanted to take you out," he placed his hands in his pockets. I was gonna say yes, but I thought about how Kenzie did me and changed my mind. I owed his ass nothing.

"Nope, I'm single," I grinned and so did he.

"Cool, put your number in my phone shorty," he handed over his iPhone and I quickly put my number in. I handed his phone back to him, and he nodded at the screen before locking it. "I'm gonna hit you up soon so we can go eat or something," he smirked with his cute ass.

"I'll be looking forward to that, Christian," I smiled and he licked his lips.

"Gorgeous," he commented before walking off.

I was smiling from ear to ear as I made my way to my car. I was kind of excited to go on this date with that guy. Shoot, I was excited about texting his ass, because at the moment I wanted some companionship. I'd never been with anyone other than Kenzie, and it was exhilarating to get to know someone else for a change.

My phone ringing snapped me from my thoughts, and I saw it was Kenzie. I rolled my eyes because Christian had me feeling myself at the moment.

"What?" I answered with an attitude.

"I'm by the gym, are you still coming?" he asked.

"Yeah," I replied dryly and hung up before he could say anything.

I was having another mood swing. Sometimes I would be so miserable that I would feel like running to Kenzie. Other days I would be on my Destiny's Child independent woman shit and be over it. Right now I was feeling like Beyoncé, but I promised him I would meet him so I was gonna go.

I drove over closer to the gym, because I was not gonna walk over there. I parked as closely as I could, and then started towards it. I spotted Kenzie sitting outside, and he looked so fine as usual. His short curly hair was freshly cut, his dark caramel complexion was so prepossessing, and his lean muscular frame was sexy as hell.

As soon as I neared him, he stood up and pulled me into his arms. His cologne smelled so good, and his arms felt like home around my body. He pulled away and pressed his lips against mine. I let him and then jumped back once I came to my senses. Why did this feel so good, when it was wrong for me to allow him to touch me in anyway?

"Talk," I spat.

"Shannon what's going on with us? I mean are we working to get back together or are you trying to move on?" He frowned down at me.

"I don't know Kenzie," I looked down at my feet.

"You don't know," he repeated. "I mean do you love me still?" he inquired.

"What did you have to tell me?" I quizzed in order to dodge his question. Hell yeah I loved his stupid ass. I loved him so fucking much, but I didn't need him knowing that. I wanted him to think that I was over him.

"Well about a month ago, I found out who Rosalind's baby's father was," he said.

"What?" I was so confused.

"Yeah, Kendrin saw her and the nigga, and the guy has been with her for six, well seven months now if they're still together," he explained.

"So it wasn't your baby?" I quizzed and he shook his head no.

"Nah, she was just doing dirt. She had a boyfriend *and* she let Kendrin smash," he dropped a bomb. *That's where I knew that bitch from! She was at that party smiling all in Kendrin's face!* I thought to myself.

"Wow, I guess you guys both were doing dirt," I said.

"Yeah, she was being neglected that's why," he said.

"Neglected?" I cocked my head.

"Yes, I was with you all the time; where I wanted to be, so it's no surprise she did what she did," he replied.

"How'd you come to that conclusion, Kenzie?" I put my hand on my hip.

"My mother," he smirked with his cute self.

"I figured. I knew you didn't figure that out on your own," I said and we chuckled.

"So Shannon, I mean, can we start working to get back to where we were?" he stared into my eyes. His green eyes were so dark and alluring.

"Kenzie, just because the baby wasn't yours doesn't change anything. You played me, and for a fucking year," I hissed. I felt myself getting furious all over again.

"Shan, I know baby, but I'm trying to make it up to you. At least come out with me," he offered.

"Fine, but I will have to let you know when I'm free," I spat and then rushed off not wanting to hear his response. When I looked back he was staring at me with his mouth open, astonished.

"I love you!" he shouted to me, but I didn't bother to respond back.

I was happy as hell that Rosalind wasn't pregnant by Kenzie, but the fact remains the same, he dogged me out. Plus, I kind of wanted to see what Christian was talking about.

A COUPLE DAYS LATER...

I'd just come home from having a nice dinner with my father, and boy was I stuffed. I missed going out with my dad, and I guess because I was so wrapped up in Kenzie, we never really got to hang out anymore.

I walked into my room, ready to gather some stuff I needed for a bubble bath. I was hoping to just relax tonight and watch some TV. I didn't want to think about Kenzie, or Rosalind, or her baby at all. I just wanted to take a moment for myself, and give my mental a break.

As I packed my shower caddy with the things that I would need, I heard my phone chime. I rolled my eyes because I knew it was probably Kenzie asking about the date I said I'd let him take me on.

+1 (410) 555-3157: *Hey beautiful, it's Chris.*

I smiled when I saw the text, because I had completely forgotten about his cute ass since I hadn't been to the class I met him at, since I met him. I stored his number, and then finished gathering my toiletries.

I took all my stuff into the bathroom, and ran a bubble bath. I grabbed my iPhone, and then dipped my body into the nice hot water.

Me: *Hey, what's up?*

Christian: *Nothing much, what are you doing?*

Me: *Watching television.*

I lied because I didn't want the conversation to turn sexual, by me letting him know I was in the bathtub.

Christian*: Cool, so how was your weekend?*

I text Christian all night until two in the morning, and I must say it felt good to talk to someone else. It's not like I was looking for a new man just yet, but talking to people sure felt great.

I NEEDED to get some paperwork filed in my office at Kingin', and I'd been here all day damn near. I got here around 8am, and it was now around 8pm, so a nigga was tired as hell. Since it was hitting prime-time, niggas were starting to pile into the strip club area, so I wanted to get out, go home, eat, get some pussy, and knock the fuck out.

As I was putting the last few papers away after double-checking my books, I heard a knock at my office door.

"Come in," I called out.

Diana walked in smiling, and then closed the door behind her. She looked real nice today, and I hated that I noticed. Her long dark hair was up in a bun on her head, and the black pencil skirt she wore seemed to be hugging her thick hips more than usual. She had on a V-neck top, and her cleavage was on full display. Visions of the times I fucked her invaded my mind, and I massaged my temples to get rid of them.

"Hey boss, that guy is back to see you again," she said.

"What guy?" I furrowed my brows.

"The guy from last time, who you told to give his information to me," she reminded me.

"Oh that nigga, umm, you know what, send him up here because I'm gonna leave out the back way," I told her and she nodded.

"You need anything else before I go," she looked into my eyes. Diana was bad as hell, and the pussy was just as good.

"No, but thank you," I cleared my throat. She nodded and then turned around to leave, making sure I got a nice lengthy glimpse of her super fat ass. "Behave nigga," I told my dick who was trying to get back up in Diana. I shut down my computer, and a few minutes later a light knock was made on my door. "Come in," I called out and stood up. Diana entered, and in walked that guy right behind her. "Send Bolo or Blade in here," I told Diana and she nodded. Blade entered the room and began to pat and check this nigga to make sure he wasn't wearing a wire or anything. I knew he had no weapons, because they checked that at the door. "Thanks B," I said.

"You're welcome, boss," he exited the room.

"Have a seat, uh what's your name again? My bad," I asked him.

"No problem man, it's TJ," he replied and shook my hand. I sat down and waited for him to be seated as well.

"Okay, so what are you looking to do out here in Baltimore?" I questioned and leaned back a little in my chair.

"I'm trying to put in some work," he stated the obvious.

"That's a given, but where? What history do you have working with shit like this? Are you more of an in house type of nigga? Like do you cook or do you kill?" I asked. His expression showed me he was confused and green as hell in this department.

"I guess I'm more of an in house type of person," he responded hoping to sound like he knew what he was talking about. I'd already peeped game though. I was gonna shoot some easy questions his way, and if he couldn't get those then I knew I was right.

"Okay, so if you see someone that you serve regularly, and they tell you to loan them some product and that they will pay double next time, what do you do? Would you try and keep that customer by giving them what they want? Or would you stick the rules, no matter the outcome?" I gave him the scenario, then clasped my hands together and leaned back in my chair to wait for his answer.

"Well, I wanna keep him around, you know. Loyalty means every damn thing so I'd loan it to him," he said trying to sound hood.

It was almost laughable. It was laughable that he thought he was a thug, that he thought that was a good answer, and ultimately that he thought he could work for me with that mouse ass attitude.

"No, that's wrong homie. You don't give any fucking loans. I don't care if that muthafucka usually asks for you personally to purchase from, if they ain't got it you don't give it," I stated sternly and he nodded.

"If someone tries to rob the house, do you give them whatever they're asking for or fight until the end?" I asked him one more, trying to give him the benefit of the doubt.

"I-I'm not sure about that one man," he said and I shook my head.

"When you work for me you better fight tooth and nail for my bread, or you'll never see the light of day again," I leaned in and he nodded quickly. "By saying that, TJ I don't think you'd be a great fit for my operation. I think you'd do great in customer service though. I know it's appealing to work for me because you make a lot of money, but you're not cut out for it. You couldn't even get the easy questions right," I said. It was so hard not to laugh in this nigga's face right now.

"Give me one more-"

"Nah, I've made my decision. Go apply at Burger King or something," I cut him off.

"Everybody don't know everything man! I'm sure you didn't know all this shit when you first got on," he hissed.

"Oh yes the fuck I did. My dad spent years grooming me and refused to pass down anything until I knew all the muthafuckin' ins and outs of this shit! Now I've made my decision and you're keeping me from going on about my day," I spat and stood up. He stood up as well, twisting his mouth and contracting his fists like he was about to do something. "You don't wanna go there with me," I told him just in case he was thinking about it. "Cause if you do, not only will you get a mud puddle stomped off in your ass, but that Burger King you thinking about won't even hire you," I added.

"Oh, that's how much clout you got?" he sneered.

"You should know I do, that's why your ass is in here begging like a bitch over a job you ain't meant for," I replied. He chuckled then inhaled sharply, before turning around and leaving angrily. "Bitch ass nigga," I said. I heard a knock, and then Diana walked back in. She handed me a glass of Bourbon, and I took it straight to the head. "Thanks shorty," I said.

"Anything for you," she rubbed my bicep and then switched out. *Damn*, I thought. *It ain't worth it man, you know Gianna will leave you,* I told myself.

I PULLED up to my crib, and walked in the house to the smell of chicken. I strolled to the kitchen and saw it was a plate of fried chicken, mashed potatoes, and creamed spinach covered with saran wrap. I'd text Gianna on my way home to tell her I was almost here, so I guess that's why she prepared the plate for me.

"Thank you, baby," I said even though she wasn't in here. I scarfed down the food, and then grabbed some juice from the fridge and downed it.

I went upstairs, and when I walked in I saw Gianna knocked out in the bed. She was wearing a little pink nightgown, and my dick was ready and willing. I could see up her smooth thighs, and her pussy through her panties.

I stripped out of my clothes, and then climbed in bed with her. Since the covers were pushed down, I assumed position between her legs, and pushed up her gown a little. I pulled on her tight boy shorts, and my mouth watered at the anticipation of eating her pussy. I got them to her knees, and then lifted her legs in the air to start. I didn't even feel like getting them past her feet.

"KJ," she said groggily. I latched my mouth onto her pussy and began flicking my tongue over her clit. "Aaa, aaahh, KJ," she whimpered. I pressed her thighs against her stomach very gently, and kept attacking her center like an animal. "Oh my gosh babe," she cried out as her pussy got wetter and wetter against my tongue. I reached up and pulled her panties from her knees, to her feet, and off, and then spread her legs wide. I dipped my tongue into her hole, and fucked her with it for a couple moments as she called out. I then trailed my tongue back up to her clit, and sucked on it softly. "I'm gonna cum, ahhh uuuh, aaahh," she squealed and then gushed into my mouth. I locked her legs in my arms, and kept going ham like I hadn't ate in forever. "KJaaayyyyy!" she screamed in a high-pitched voice as her legs trembled violently. I didn't care; I was still hungry. She propped herself up using her elbows, and watched me with her pretty face scrunched. "Mmmm, uuuuhh, uuuh, babyyyyy!" she yelped and massaged my head. "Don't pull away, give it to me," I demanded when she tried to run. She pushed her pussy into my mouth, and I went in on her clit. "Uggghhhh!" she grunted in her cute little voice as she exploded again, wetting the sheets under herself. I could do that shit all day.

I kissed her lower lips a couple times very gently, and then up her small belly. She laid there panting heavily, as I lifted her gown up and off.

"I love eating that pussy," I said before tonguing her down for a little bit.

I laid on my back, and then pulled her on top of me, but with her back to me. I placed her legs on the outside of mine so they'd be nice and open, and then pushed her down onto my dick. She tried to sit up and ride me backwards but I stopped her. I liked this position because I could control how wide her legs stayed open for me, and how fast we went. I started slowly going in and out of her, while groping her breasts and kissing on the back of her neck as she whimpered. I then caressed her smooth thighs, as I started to speed up a bit. I could feel her back drenching with sweat up against my chest.

"My pussy is so good, oh fuck," I groaned in her ear before sucking on it.

"Aaah, uuhh," she clenched her teeth together and smashed her hand into the bed. She had no control and it was bliss. I could make her cum as many times as I wanted. "Mmmmm!" She pursed her lips together and I felt her burst on my dick.

"Damn, that's three," I whispered and craned my neck around to suck her lips as she called out.

I sped up my pelvic thrusts while toying with her clit, and she came again soon after. I slowed down to give her a mini break, and let my hands roam her body as I pleased. I started going ham again, and we both exploded.

"Fuck," I called out and sucked her bottom lip again. She was soaking with sweat, to where it looked like someone had thrown a bucket of water on her. I pulled her up to let my dick fall out, and then picked her legs up so she could move. She rolled off of onto the side and glared at me. "What?" I laughed.

"Don't fuck me like that!" she pouted.

"Why? You came so many times." I was cracking up.

"Because I can't do anything but-"

"Take this dick and that's what I wanted. I'm gon' fuck yo ass like that all the time. And I went easy because of the baby, so imagine when he's out," I kissed her soft lips. She just frowned even more, making it funnier.

"Putting me in these circus positions!" She hopped out of the bed and stormed to the bathroom. I followed her so we could go at it again. Ha ha.

I WAS SITTING in my hotel room, fuming. The way that nigga dissed me had me hotter than fish grease. I wanted to slap the shit out of him for coming at me the way he did, but a part of me knew that was a fight I may lose.

You may recognize my name, but then again you may not, so let me tell you a little about myself. I was born here in Baltimore, but I was raised in Atlanta, Georgia by my grandmother. By the time I was born, my father had already been murdered by his so called best friend Kendrick King; yes, KJ's father. Because my mother couldn't afford to raise me on her own without my dad, she had to send me down South with my granny. Before I could even make it to my first birthday, my mother was murdered as well, and take a wild guess who pulled it off; Kendrick King again.

I hated this nigga because he took my parents before a nigga even got a chance to knowingly meet them, and for what? He and my dad were thick as thieves according to my grandmother, so how and why did this nigga kill him? I'm willing to bet that nigga was jealous of my father, and that's what my grandma felt too.

I couldn't just sit back and allow this nigga to get away with killing both of my fucking parents; I just couldn't. I had to do this for them, and for my grandma. This nigga and his brother's killed all of her kids, and she wasn't equipped to get revenge herself, but that's what I was here for. She told me to be careful, and to try and get a picture of my cousin Kennedy for her.

Kennedy was my aunt Adrienne's daughter that she had with Kendrick King's brother Kendon. They claim that she overdosed, but my grandma believes they killed her too.

So why am I coming for Kendrick Jr. and not the original? Well there are two reasons for that. One is because I honestly don't think I could take Kendrick Sr., and I didn't come here to die. Secondly, because getting over on his son would hurt him just the way he hurt me by taking my parents.

"So what happened babe?" my girlfriend Shalyssa came from the bathroom, and laid down in one of the twin beds. We were staying at the Country Inn by the airport in Linthicum Heights.

"Nigga came at me foul," I scoffed and twisted open a new bottle of Pinnacle.

"So now that he ain't gon' let you on, what's the plan?" she asked.

"I'm gonna try to get one of the others to put me on. He has a brother and cousin working with him," I smiled and looked over at her. She wasn't smiling back; instead she had a worried look on her face. "Fuck wrong with you?" I spat.

"I just don't know about this Trenton, I mean we didn't really plan it well," she sat up on the bed and fidgeted. "I told you we need a team."

"Would you quit with that? This is KJ, not the original Kendrick, we'll be good," I assured her and sipped my vodka straight. "We don't need a fucking team to kill one nigga."

"TJ, I've heard he's the same and maybe even a little crazier," she looked into my eyes. She was pissing me off acting all scared and shit like I couldn't protect her.

"Well, I don't believe it. And you ain't made no fucking progress on befriending their bitches!" I barked.

"I know, babe, I've been trying to think of an angle. I can't just come up to them and start trying to be friends," she shrugged and poked out her full lips.

"Well the money we stole from my grandma is starting to dwindle, so maybe you should try and get a job at Kingin' or something," I told her.

"And what are you gonna do for money?" she raised a brow.

"Working for Kendrick Jr.," I said and refilled my glass.

"But TJ, he already said he wont-"

"Well someone else will! I will get in on their shit and do what the fuck I need to do to get back at this nigga, all the while getting some money! You take care of your fucking part and let me do mine! Stop being so fucking scared of this nigga ma! I ain't gone let shit happen to you aight? I would die first," I said.

"Why didn't you just kill him at the job interview?" she squinted her eyes. "You could've just killed him so we could be on our way!"

"Because I couldn't bring any weapons in! You think it's that easy to touch that nigga? You have to be prepared, and wait until he's alone or out with his girl or some shit!" I roared. "If I would've shot him in his office they would've lit my ass up right after." She just nodded but I could tell her faith in me was little to nonexistent.

I didn't care though; I would just have to prove her and everybody else wrong. The King family legacy would go down in flames, even if I had to torch the shit on my damn own. Damn, my name would forever be synonymous with the nigga who took down the head honcho. KJ had better enjoy his last days while he still had them, and Kendrick Sr. better be prepared to lose his first born.

OUR TECH GUY Oscar had finally gotten information for me on the niggas that robbed my brother, so KJ and I were gonna go meet them and see what was up. I was so ready to handle these niggas, and Kendall would just have to be mad at me.

We entered the warehouse, and then went to the back to let Oscar in. He followed us to a secluded room, and Bolo closed and stood by the door.

"Alright what you got?" I asked. I was anxious as fuck.

"The people that threw coffee on your girl's shoes *are* the same people that robbed your brother. We got someone to get info from the inside on them, which is how we were able to connect the two. Basically they're a crew named Porn Stars, and Brice was a part of them. They're like a criminal gang, so they go around robbing people and shit, nothing major. But they do have plans for both of y'all," Oscar explained. "They're really upset about Brice disappearing."

"Porn Stars? Who the fuck came up with that shit?" KJ chuckled and so did I.

"Yeah, that's what I said, but so far they're trying to get back at you two and Aysia for setting Brice up," Oscar responded and then pulled out pictures to show us what they looked like.

"A bunch of busted ass niggas and bitches," KJ commented and the three of us died laughing. He pulled out a paper and said, "Here is a list of places that they usually hang out at."

"Thanks man," I said and he nodded.

"You're welcome, anytime boss," Oscar stood to his feet. After Bolo escorted him out, KJ and I got to talking.

"So let's just spray these niggas. They're not a fucking gang dawg, they're a clique," KJ suggested.

"You're right, they're stupid enough to hang at the same places all together while making threats at the same time," I shook my head at how dumb they were.

"Exactly, don't make threats when you know you're not even smart enough to switch up your damn whereabouts. Plus, what are they gonna do? Jump us?" we chuckled in unison.

"Alright, so yeah, we can spray them when they're all hanging outside of this house." I pointed to the picture that showed them chilling on the porch of a crib in Coppin Heights.

"I mean these muthafuckas are so beneath me that I'm thinking we should have the little homies spray their asses. They should be able to handle it," KJ said. "And that way Kendall won't feel like we saved him, because *we* ain't do it," he smiled and so did I.

"That's why I fuck with you," I dapped him up. I couldn't wait to get confirmation of this little clique's death.

"That's why the bitches do too," he cracked and we snickered.

"Nigga you better not let Gigi hear you say that shit," I hit his arm.

"Yeah I know. She already be about to stab me with butter knives and shit when I even look at another girl. I went to get my car from valet, and she swore I was grinning in the valet chicks face," he bucked his eyes as I cackled. "She tried to walk her pregnant ass home because she didn't want to get in the car. I had to sit and beg my shorty for twenty minutes to get in the fucking car with me before she finally did," he continued as I laughed hard as hell.

"I think it's them hormones," I nodded with a smile.

"I know it is, because she never acted like that. But it's cool, that's my baby," he said and stood up. "She's carrying my son, so I can let her act a fool for the time being," he smiled.

"Oh, you guys found out the sex?" I quizzed and stood up as well.

"Nah, but I only make boys," he nodded and I laughed at his ass.

After I parted ways with KJ, I wanted to talk to Aysia and let her know my assumptions were correct. She swore that I was just being paranoid, so I couldn't wait to burst her little bubble.

I found her coming out of the bathroom with some music playing from her iPad.

"Hey beautiful," I smirked.

"Hey," she cut the music off and then let her towel fall.

I licked my lips at the sight of her pecan complexion, sexy frame, and perfectly trimmed pussy. Although pregnant, she was still very sexy to me. As soon as she neared me I kissed her gently. She started to unbuckle my pants, and then dropped to her knees.

"You know I was right about what happened to you and Kendall," I looked down at her.

"For real?" she stood up.

"Yes, but it's gonna be taken care of by tomorrow night," I assured her.

I pulled my shirt off along with the rest of my clothing, and then pushed Aysia onto the bed. I put her on all fours, and then dropped down to lick her pussy from the back.

"Mmmm," she purred. I gripped her ass cheeks, and spread them so I could literally lick her up and down. "Kaleeini, baby," she moaned loudly as I sucked on her clit. I smacked her ass, and she pressed her face into the bed. That gave me more access, and I began feasting on her harder until she released. I stood up, and then rubbed the head of my dick along the length of her dripping pussy.

"You are so wet, shorty," I said before plunging into her. I had to pause for a second to make sure I didn't nut immediately. I gripped her small waist, and began moving slowly in and out of her tight walls. "Shit," I commented.

"You feel so good," she cooed and balled the sheets in her fists. I started pulling out slowly, and going in fast making her whimper like a kitten.

"Oh damn," I pursed my lips at how good she felt. I sped up some more, watching her small round ass bounce, and a smile spread across my face.

"Aaah, aaah, aaaah, aaahh!" she called out with every powerful stroke I delivered, killing the pussy every time. "I uuuuh I-" I don't know what the fuck she was trying to say, but I felt her drench my dick so I went even harder in the paint.

"Ugggghh," I growled as I filled her up. I wound my hips slowly before pulling out, and she turned around to lie on her back.

"I love you," she panted and pulled me down between her legs. I moved my fingers around in her wetness as we kissed hungrily.

"I love you too, shorty."

I could finally stop worrying about my brothers and girl, because now them niggas would be gone in no time.

KJ WASN'T ANSWERING his phone, and we were supposed do our registry at Target in an hour and a half. I hated when he let his work come before everything else in his life, but I guess that was what I signed up for.

I gathered all my things and then went downstairs so I could go find him. I did not feel like driving because this belly was getting bigger and heavier, but desperate times called for desperate measures. It's almost like I blew up overnight though, and I was hoping it stopped growing soon.

I climbed into my BMW that KJ purchased me, and then headed to Kingin'. I knew that was probably where he was, and that pissed me off even more. I swear he better be in his office and not downstairs watching bitches shake their fake asses.

On the way there, I called him again just to see if he would answer this time but he didn't. About twenty minutes later I was pulling into the back parking lot of Kingin', and hopping out angrily as fuck. I walked my ass right up to the front, not caring if people were waiting to get inside. It was around 6:45pm because KJ said he couldn't do the registry stuff until after 7pm.

"Hello," the bouncer said and looked me up and down.

I was a little irritated that Bolo wasn't working the door because he knew me. However, Bolo was a personal worker for KJ, Kaleeini, and Kendrin, not Kingin', so he only did certain events.

"Yes, I need to get in there and speak with my boyfriend," I responded as I took in his wide frame.

"Who is your boyfriend?" he chuckled at me like I was the funniest joke. The question caught me off guard, but I wanted to stay as calm as possible.

"KJ, nigga," I spat. I couldn't believe he didn't know who I was! It would've been different if it was before we made things official, but shit I had his baby in my body!

"Did-"

"Look, I'm pregnant as I'm sure you can see, hungry, and tired, and I don't have time for you to be bouncer of the fucking year, aight?" I hissed and he bucked his eyes, which my freshly done mink nail almost poked out. He was one of those buff but short niggas.

He said something into his headset, and I tried to walk by but he stopped me. I wanted to take off on his ass, but the odds were obviously against me. I stood there tapping my foot, furious as I watched all the people waiting to get inside and have fun.

"What's the fucking hold up!" I screamed at the bouncer.

"I'm waiting for confirmation," he said dryly. I could tell he thought I was another crazy groupie trying to claim KJ, which pissed me off. I pulled out my phone to dial KJ again, when his worker Blade emerged. He must've heard me yelling, because he wore a confused expression on his face.

"You okay, Gigi?" Blade asked and the ugly ass bouncer's eyes bucked.

"No, I'm trying to get in and see KJ, but Bear in the Big Blue House won't let me by," I hung up the phone, and folded my arms after adjusting my Birkin bag.

"Nigga what the fuck is you doing at the door and you don't even know who to let by? That's Kendrick's baby mama," Blade explained.

I didn't like that title, but I would take fuck buddy right now if it meant I could get in.

"Oh man, I totally forgot. I didn't have the list on me," he said as Blade waved me over.

I saw some girls sizing me up once they heard who I was, and I got even angrier at the fact that I wasn't dressed up to stunt on these hoes. They were dressed real nice in expensive brands, including the type of weave in their heads. I had on black tights, some gray Yeezy Boost 350's that KJ just got me, and a gray crew neck. My hair was in a ponytail, so nothing special. I did make sure to floss that big ass diamond KJ had given me though, as I walked into the club.

I immediately started towards KJ's office, and Blade jogged a little to catch up to me.

"Be careful shorty, these niggas can get rowdy. Your man will kill me if something happens to you," he said but I declined to respond. He sure wasn't acting like he gave a fuck about me right now.

We got to KJ's office, which was upstairs and down a narrow hall, and some light skinned chick was walking out. She was dressed like she worked at the bar but I didn't give a fuck. She was pretty with big titties and a big butt, two things KJ loved. My chest heaved up and down as I watched her switch past Blade and I. These hormones had me on one.

"Hellooo," she sang and floated off. *She better not have gotten any of my dick*, I thought.

I pushed the already open door further open, and there KJ was, sitting at his desk. Blade gave him a look as if he was saying *I wouldn't wanna be you right now*, and then he left, closing the door behind him.

"Hey beautiful, what you doing here?" KJ grinned.

"That's what the fuck I'm trying to figure out about you, nigga. Did you forget about the registry?" I dropped my bag on his desk and folded my arms.

"Oh damn, low key I did forget because-"

"I don't wanna hear it, KJ. And who is that bitch that came

floating out of here with a glow like she just got some dick?" I grimaced.

"That's Diana, she's the manager, remember?" He burst into laughter. He was so fucking sexy. I wanted to slap him yet fuck him at the same time. I needed to take a chill pill.

"What is so funny?" I furrowed my brows.

"You. Coming in here trying to check me. It's cute," he chuckled and leaned down to kiss me, and I pushed him back lightly. "Come here," he yanked me back and kissed me harder. He then pecked me a couple times before loosening his grip on my arm.

"Your bitch ass doorman had me waiting outside for the longest and wouldn't let me by! These niggas don't know who I am by now, KJ? And then you got Blade calling me your baby mama-"

"Calm down, Gianna. Baby, sit down and relax. You hungry? I can have them bring some fries and strips up here," he offered and I turned my head.

"Yes, I will take some fries," I responded begrudgingly. I didn't want to want what he offered, but I was a little hungry.

"Okay, I will be right back. Do not move your little pretty self from this spot, okay?" He looked down at me and I nodded.

I waited for a few moments, and KJ walked in with a plate of piping hot fries and chicken strips, along with a cup of apple juice.

"Thank you, baby," I cheesed.

"See, that's all your grumpy ass needed," he said as he set it in front of me.

"I just fired the door guy. I'm sorry about that, aight?" he said and I just shook my head yes because my mouth was full. "Oh, Diana got this gift for you," he picked a little gift bag up off his desk and handed it to me.

I wiped my hands off after rolling my eyes, and then took it. I reached in and it was a tube of belly balm. I frowned at it and looked up at KJ.

"She said it'll keep you from having stretch marks on your stomach," he smiled like it was such a nice gift.

"You tell that bitch to keep it for her nasty ass and hips!" I barked and his eyes bucked. "I don't want no fucking belly cream! I don't need her reminding me of stretch marks!" I threw the balm back in the bag as KJ laughed. He then sat next to me and kissed my cheek.

"You know when you act like that you make my dick so hard," he whispered in my ear, and reached his hand down into my new maternity tights. I was about to bite my fry, but he took it out of my hand, and slipped his tongue into my mouth.

"Only a quickie because we have to go-"

"Shut up," he said and started to push my tights and panties down, while sucking my lips.

SHANNON, Gianna, Willow, and I were at the nail shop and my feet were in dire need of the work. I'd been too lazy to come, but now that my shit had started to chip it was a must. I was so embarrassed when Kaleeini asked me when was I was going to get my feet done.

I smiled as I looked at the outside, because the sun was finally starting to come out more. It was still pretty breezy, but not like before and I was thankful. I knew soon enough I'd be able to wear my short shorts and tube tops again.

The four of us were directed to our specific massage chairs, and I swear I heard my feet exhale once they hit the hot water with the jet massagers. Toni Braxton's "Breathe Again" lyrics circled my mind as I stared down at my pitiful dogs.

"I needed this," Gianna sighed, seemingly reading my mind. "KJ bought me a massager at home, but I still needed this professional treatment."

"Me too, girl. My feet are hurting a lot more lately. My mom said the baby will do that though," I sighed as I thought about it.

"Speaking of babies, I have some stuff to tell you guys," Shannon smirked. I hadn't seen her smirk or smile since Willow's wedding tasting.

"What? You know I love gossip!" Willow smiled with her messy ass.

We were the only people in the shop, so I guess that's why Shannon felt it was okay to spill some information while in public.

"So about a week and a half ago, Kenzie told me he found out he wasn't the father of that chick Rosalind's baby. Some other nigga that she's been dating for the past seven months was," she looked at us and all of our jaws were on the damn floor.

"Wait, so she lied this whole time?" I questioned to be sure I heard her correctly.

"Yes bitch. I was happy he told me, but it still doesn't change the fact that he had another girlfriend the whole time we dated," she shook her head as she watched the nail lady take the polish off of her toenails.

"Yeah that's true," Gianna chimed in.

"And I don't know if you remember, but do you recall the girl that was dancing on Kendrin at Tasha's party awhile back?" Shannon looked at Willow and she nodded nervously. I was wondering why she seemed to feel uneasy. "Well, that's the same girl, and apparently Kendrin smashed her too," she looked at Willow. I was waiting for her to blow up like a muthafucka, but she didn't move.

"Willow, did you hear what she said?" I stuck my neck out so that I could see her face better, since Shannon and Gianna were sitting in between us.

"Okay, so I already knew that she slept with Kendrin. She approached me and Gianna at the gym, and tried to say she was pregnant by Kendrin," Willow admitted.

"What the fuck!" Shannon and I both said in unison.

Gianna's ass was quiet as she munched on some peanut butter crackers, so I knew her ass must've known.

"So that's why your ass was so depressed and no one knew why," Shannon smacked her lips and shook her head.

"Why didn't you tell us?" I frowned.

"Because I was embarrassed! I thought he for real got her pregnant, but he told me he didn't and that he was for sure. I believed him, and I'm happy he was telling the truth," she replied.

"Wait so you knew she was pregnant or saying she was pregnant by Kenzie?" Shannon glared at Willow.

"No, bitch! He just said that he wasn't the father, and he was one hundred percent positive," she said.

"So Kendrin knew that Kenzie possibly had a baby by another girl?" I asked and she nodded.

"He knew but he didn't tell me that shit. I had no idea that it was the same bitch claiming to be pregnant by Kendrin until you found out about her, I swear. That's when Kendrin admitted it to me," Willow held her hands up in mock surrender.

"And Gianna, what's your excuse for not mentioning that Rosalind was the same bitch that pinned a baby on Kendrin?" I asked.

"Willow told me not to tell anyone when Rosalind initially approached her, so I wasn't about to be getting into that. I knew Shannon would find out it was the same bitch sooner or later. But be mad at them niggas, they've known for the longest," she responded.

"I swear them niggas are shady," Shannon scoffed.

"That's his cousin though Shan, you can't expect him to step on his toes, not unless it's some life or death shit," Willow said.

"Yeah, that is true. If one of y'all were cheating I wouldn't tell," I grinned and they laughed. "Nobody is cheating right?" I scanned the three of them and we all chuckled.

While we were laughing, some girl dressed to the nines walked in and stared me down. "I'm here for a fill Lina," she told the nail specialist.

"Okay honey, sit down," she responded and pointed to the chair.

She turned on the heels of her royal blue boots, and switched to her seat after giving me another stare down.

I didn't know what her problem was, but I had a feeling it was something with Brice and his Porn Star crew. I hoped Kaleeini took care of that shit already, because I was getting tired of always being stared at. Even when muthafuckas would just look at me, I would be paranoid as fuck.

When Kaleeini explained to me that Brice was a part of a clique named Porn Stars, I thought it was a damn joke. I'd never heard of that shit, and it sounded stupid as fuck. They're pretty much a group of petty criminals, who go around robbing and fucking with people for no reason. I knew Brice used to hang with big ass groups, but I just assumed it was because he was well connected throughout the hood. I would've never guessed that he was a part of some stupid shit like that.

I glanced towards the exit where the girl was waiting, and she looked at me and smirked. I took a deep breath and decided to ignore her for the rest of my visit, because if she hadn't said anything yet, then maybe she wasn't going to at all.

Once we were all done, we headed out of the nail shop. As I was passing old girl, I heard her say to her friend, "That's Kaleeini's girl."

The friend replied, "How do you know? She's not even pretty enough."

"I saw them kissing at the movies, and she's all on his Instagram," she sucked her teeth.

"And our baby is due in August," I turned around and smiled while rubbing my small bump.

I didn't care if they couldn't see it that well. They just stared at me, clearly caught off guard that I'd heard their little conversation. Stupid ass bitches. I was happy that they weren't from Brice's crew, but it just reminded me of how many bitches wanted to ride Kaleeini Express. I would shank a bitch for my nigga though, so they'd better tread lightly.

"What was that about?" Shannon asked as we all got into Willow's car.

"Some bitches whispering and shit about Kaleeini like I can't hear their ghetto asses," I smacked my lips and reached for my seatbelt.

"What did they say?" Gianna quizzed.

"Just pointing me out saying I wasn't cute enough to be his girl and shit. Clearly he doesn't agree, because I got the keys to the crib, a new whip, and a baby coming," I cocked my head as they chuckled.

"Bitches are stupid over them green eyes boy," Willow shook her head as she cranked up her car.

"Well, I'm crazy over them green eyes, so they better not even dream about my nigga too much," I said and folded my arms.

"Ooh shit! This pregnant Aysia is not the one to play with," Shannon taunted and they all snickered.

"Nah, but I feel you, girl. KJ be about to turn me into Freddy Kruger on these bitches. I be ready to climb up in their beds and slice their asses up," Gianna said as we laughed.

"Please wait until you have the baby before you start slicing bitches up, okay?" Willow looked in her rearview at Gianna with a smile.

"I will see what I can do," she smirked.

I WAS at my father's club, King Brothers, watching some strippers with my cousin Drew. I hadn't been here in a while because I was too busy, but it was popping like always. I loved coming to family owned businesses, because they allowed my ass to drink.

"You want a private dance?" one of the chicks asked me as she swayed to the music.

She was standing on the outside of the VIP area smiling. She was pretty as hell, but I couldn't let her give me a dance. Somehow I felt like Willow would show up and show the fuck out, and I didn't wanna deal with that. A dance was not worth the headache whatsoever.

"Nah, I'm good shorty, but thank you," I smiled.

"I will do it for free," she licked her lips. "And anything else you want done for free," she cocked her head and Drew burst into laughter.

See how hard it was for a nigga? Like she was literally offering to do whatever I wanted right here and right now. As Kanye once said, *how he stay faithful in a room full of hoes?*

"I appreciate that, but my fiancée would be upset," I explained and she rolled her eyes with a smile.

"Your fiancée wouldn't hear it from me," she said and pretended to zip her lips.

"She's probably listening to this conversation right now," I chuckled and so did she.

"Alright baby, let me know if you change your mind," she raised a brow and turned to walk away.

"Damn," Drew commented on her humongous ass.

"That shit was ridiculous," I said agreeing with him on it.

If I was single, she wouldn't have had to ask twice at all. I would've taken her to a private room and fucked the shit out of her without even thinking about it.

As I sipped my whiskey and watched this white stripper named Snow Bunny shake her ass, the VIP bouncer tapped my shoulder.

"Young man wants to holla at you," the bouncer said and pointed to this cat standing outside of the VIP. I frowned at Drew before turning back to face the bouncer. I then turned my attention to the guy.

"What you want to talk about?" I looked down at him.

"Just a few things I can't really say out loud," he shouted back over the music.

"It's cool," I said.

The bouncer waved him up, and he jogged up the five stairs to get in here. He sat across from me and Drew after shaking our hands. He wasn't dressed like much, and I was really confused as to what the fuck he could possibly want to talk to me about.

"Talk," I said and sipped my drink again.

"I'm TJ, and you're Kendrin right?" He pointed to me and I nodded. "Well I'm trying to get down with the team you know," he grinned.

"What team?" I played dumb and then waved the waitress down to refill my glass.

"The umm, operation," he smiled and looked at Drew and me.

"You need to speak with someone else," Drew told him.

"What you mean? Don't y'all run this shit?" he scowled.

"Yes, but only certain parts. As far as deciding who gets hired on, that's someone else," I explained.

"Who? Your brother?" He looked at me and then scoffed like he had a problem with that.

"If you know who, then why are you in my face?"

"I already got at your brother and he was on some other shit," he sucked his teeth.

"Well, I don't know what to tell you bro," I shrugged as the waitress filled my glass back up as well as Drew's.

"Would you like a drink?" she asked TJ.

"Nah he's leaving this area in a little bit," I answered her before he could say anything. He was not about to be chilling up here with me, getting free drinks and shit. The waitress nodded and then turned around to leave.

"So you can't put in a good word for me?" he furrowed his brows.

"A good word? Nigga, we don't even know you, how the fuck we gon' put in a good word?" Drew turned his lip up.

"And this ain't no fucking customer service job homie, ain't shit a good word gon' do for you if my brother has already denied you," I explained.

"Come on man, help me out. I need to make some bread and fast," he pleaded with his hands in prayer mode.

"That's not my problem, man," I responded.

What the fuck did he want me to do? KJ was given complete autonomy when my dad passed the operation down to him. KJ got the last word, and my dad made sure every muthafucka knew that. What the fuck I look like stepping on my brother's toes to put some nigga on that I don't even fucking know. And I'm sure KJ didn't add him for good reason. Plus, we had enough niggas working. We didn't have too many people, which meant more money for everybody, and that's the way we liked to keep it.

"We supposed to be brothers, you can't help me out? I got a fucking family!" he shouted. *Brothers? Negro please*, I thought.

"Aye nigga, I don't know who the fuck you getting loud with, but I don' already told you I can't fucking help you. If you want my brother's mind to be changed, you ain't going about it the right fucking way. I can see why he didn't put your whining ass on. Now get the fuck out of my VIP before I'm forced to knock the shit out of you in front of all these people," I grimaced.

Like I explained before, I wasn't one to argue and bicker. Either we were fighting or you were getting the fuck out my face. All this back and forth shit wasn't my style, and he was about to find that out in one of the worst ways. This nigga was about to take me there, and I wasn't in the mood for it. He didn't want it me.

He hopped up and stormed out like the bitch that he was, and I made sure to tell the bouncer that Drew and I wouldn't be accepting any more fucking visitors. I just wanted to chill and relax, not sit up and argue with bitch boys about getting work.

I continued to party and shit, and after a while I was tipsy and ready to go home. I couldn't drive like this, so I pulled my phone out to dial Willow. I knew she was gon' be hot, but she was gon' bring that ass here and get me. Hopefully I could get some head too. I smiled to myself as I thought about it.

As I was standing in the back, listening to the line trill, I heard gunshots ring out. I looked around, just as I felt a sharp pain in my abdomen. I touched my stomach just as another shot hit my shoulder. I rushed to the back door of the club, and I heard tires screech like the person had drove off.

"Hello?" Willow answered, and I could tell that she had been asleep.

"Baby I got shot-" I could taste blood, and I knew it wasn't looking good for me.

"Kendrin, where are you?" she screamed.

My vision became cloudy, and then I fell to the ground. I listened to Willow screaming my name as everything faded to black.

"Kᴇɴᴅʀɪɴ!" I screeched into the phone again.

Kendrin had stopped responding, so I hopped up to leave. I had on a little ass nightgown but I didn't care. I slipped into my Chucks and my jacket that were by the bedroom door, and then went down the stairs.

As I walked through the foyer to the door, I logged into his iCloud so I could locate his phone. I saw the address matched King Brother's, and ran to my car fast as hell. On the way there, I dialed 911 as tears ran down my face. I gave them the address and let them know that my baby had been shot and what he looked like. *Please don't die Kendrin, I need you, I need you,* I chanted in my head

By the time I got to KB's, it was surrounded with police and ambulance trucks. I was happy they came fast, because a lot of times these muthafuckas didn't care about black males being shot. I didn't know if they were here because of the call I'd placed, or because of the call someone else may have put in. Shit whatever the reason, I was just thanking the Lord.

I parked horribly, and then ran to the scene so I could see Kendrin. I saw them wheeling him to the truck with an oxygen mask on his face, which was comforting to see. I let out a sigh of relief to see that he wasn't in a black body bag, because I would have had a heart attack right here. I couldn't function if he died.

"Can you please tell me where you're taking him?" I tugged on one of the EMT's sleeves. He turned to me and said,

"Who are you?"

"His fiancée," I panted and searched his ice blue eyes, as I waited for a response.

"We're taking him to Mercy," he half smiled and then hopped on.

I ran to my car, and got ready to follow the truck to the hospital. I was running red lights right with their asses, and no police said shit about it. I parked quickly upon arriving, and ran alongside the EMT's as they pushed my baby into the hospital.

Kendrin's once white shirt was a deep dark red color from so much blood. The sight made my stomach turn, because I didn't want him to die from losing so much.

"He's lost a lot of blood so we need to get to work on him now!" someone yelled and I tried to follow them but they stopped me.

"Just wait out here please and sign in," the nurse told me.

I did as she asked, and then went to sit down. My mind raced as I thought about my baby's fate. He had to live; he just had to. I couldn't go on if he left me here.

I texted my friends to let them know what happened so that they could tell their men. I then called Mrs. King to inform her of the news. She was very frantic and I could tell she was worried as hell about her son.

Thirty minutes went by and I was going crazy. It seemed like hours had passed because they hadn't updated me at all. Everybody started showing up at different times, and as soon as I saw my friends they hugged me tightly. Kendrae and Kendria looked worried as hell, and KJ was furious.

"Have they said anything?" Mr. King squinted his eyes while holding Nic's hand. Her face had a few tearstains just like mine.

"No, but it feels like they've been in there forever," I responded as Shannon rubbed my back gently.

"I don't understand what the fuck happened!" KJ shouted and slapped the wall with both hands. Gianna tried to console him, but I was scared he may accidently hit her stomach.

He was so angry, and I could tell he was ready to pull his gun out and shoot anybody right about now.

Kendrin's father was visibly angry as well, but I knew he was keeping calm in order to make sure Nic was okay. Mr. King sat down, and then pulled Nic into his lap.

"He's gonna be okay," he said in a low tone, and Nic kissed his lips.

He tightened his grip around her waist, and laid his head against her chest. She caressed his head after adjusting herself in his lap and letting out a huge sigh. I watched them and hoped that I would be able to have Kendrin show me love like that. He just needed to make it.

We sat and waited for three hours, until the doctor finally came out looking for Kendrin's family. Since I wasn't exactly his family yet, his mother and father were the ones the doctor talked to. I waited impatiently for them to come back and let us know what was up, while praying that Kendrin was okay.

I stood up as soon as I saw Nic hit the corner, and waited for her to speak. "So he's gonna be okay, thank God. They got the bullets out and the shooter missed any vital organs, so he's not in too bad of a shape. He's in a medically induced coma though, so they don't wanna let anyone see him but me and his father, and siblings can as well," she explained and I tried to contain my tears. "He can have non familial visits tomorrow."

I was tempted to yell "I want to see him now" but instead, I just nodded my head, hugged everyone, and then left out. I didn't wanna be here if I couldn't see him. I wanted to go home and sleep the hours away, so that I could wake up and run back down here.

I COULD BARELY SLEEP, so when my alarm rang at 9am, I was able to hop up quickly. I rushed off to the shower, and as soon as I was finished, I brushed my teeth, grabbed a banana, and then sped to the hospital. I hoped Kendrin was awake now, because I needed to hear his voice to be sure that he was okay.

After checking in, I was able to see my baby, since Mrs. King had me on the list of people that were able to see him. When I walked into his room, Nic was sitting there with him, and they both smiled when they saw me. My heart started beating normally again, knowing my man was alive and well. Even though Nic had told us last night that he was good, seeing him look me in the eyes was what I needed to feel better about it all.

"Hi, honey. I'm gonna leave so you can have him to yourself," Nic grinned. She kissed Kendrin's face, and then stared down at him for a little bit.

"Thank you," I giggled and hugged her once she neared me.

I watched her leave, and then I closed the door behind her. As soon as I turned back to see Kendrin, a smile was on both of our faces. His smile was weak but I didn't care. I could still see his dimples sitting deeply in his cheeks.

"Come here," he said. I could see he was in pain with every word that he spoke.

I walked over to him, and leaned down to kiss him softly. I wasn't quite sure where he was shot, and I didn't want to apply pressure to the wounds.

"You still look sexy even though you're all shot up in this bed," I smiled and so did he.

"Thank you. I was hoping I still looked sexy lying here," he joked and cleared his throat.

He pressed the button on the remote so that he was able to sit up a little. He winced in pain as the back of the bed began to lift. I held tightly onto his free hand, as he positioned himself the way he wanted.

"I'm so happy you're alive, baby," I whispered as I caressed his fade. I felt like I was about to cry, and I was trying to hold back the tears.

"Me too. I would hate to leave without marrying you first," he bit his lip and then stared off at the wall like he was thinking.

"You shouldn't be thinking about that," I chuckled and rubbed his fresh fade.

"Well I am. I thought I was a goner, and all I could think about was how we didn't get married first," he responded as he continued to stare at the wall straight ahead.

"I love you, Kendrin," I smirked and craned my neck around so that I could see his pretty seaweed colored eyes.

"I love you more shorty, and as soon as I get out of here we need to make that happen," he looked at me seriously.

"What about my cake? It won't be ready for four months," I exclaimed. I had to have that cake!

"We can still have a wedding, but we can go to justice of the peace or some shit to get the marriage done now," he grabbed my small hand in his.

"Okay," I pecked his mouth a couple times, and then our lips parted to introduce our tongues. *Thank you God*, I thought.

TWO NIGHTS LATER...

I was ready as hell to get my girl back. It'd been too damn long, and the wait was gonna end tonight. She'd agreed to let me take her on a date, and after brushing me off for a few weeks, she finally was about to make good on her word. I just hoped she knew that after tonight, there would be no more fucking games.

I was taking her to her favorite place, Fogo de Chao on Pratt Street. It was a Brazilian restaurant that Shannon was obsessed with and always wanted to go to. I wanted to bring her there not only because she loved it, but also because I wanted to remind her of the great times we had together.

I fastened my chain around my neck, and then grabbed my phone to text her that I was on my way. I kissed my mom goodbye when I saw her in the foyer, and then hurried to the door.

"Good luck, Kenzie," my little sister Kendlie said to me, making my mom chuckle.

"I won't need it, but thanks," I smirked and pulled the huge front door open. I closed the door behind me, and then said a quick prayer to God before rushing to my car to get to Shannon.

When I pulled up, I checked my appearance once more, and then got out to go inside of her apartment building. This was the first time I was gonna be face to face with her dad since that little incident with Rosalind, and nervous was an understatement.

I knocked on the door, and took a deep breath to prepare myself. The door came open, and there stood Mr, Breaux- Shannon's father. He was wearing some jeans that must have been thirty years old, and a t-shirt with Martin Luther King Jr. on it. His gray beard was a bit scruffier than usual, and his brown skin seemed to be darker than before.

"Good evening sir, I'm here to pick Shannon up," I smiled and he just stared at me. He didn't say anything, so I cleared my throat because the silence was awkward.

"Come in Kenzie, and sit down," he said and gestured towards the couch. I walked in and sat down like he'd asked me to, and inhaled sharply while wondering what was next.

"Daddy who-" Shannon came out and stopped when she saw me.

I could see a smile threatening to burst through her face, but she didn't wanna show it. She wasn't finished dressing, but she looked so pretty anyway. Damn, I missed my shorty something crazy.

"Go back to your room Shannon, I wanna talk to Kenzie for a bit before you leave," he told her and I was sweating bullets.

I wasn't trying to talk to him, because I knew it would be all bad. I didn't want him telling me I couldn't date his daughter or some shit like that, because we were gonna have some problems. Mr. Breaux had always been fond of me, and I hated that our relationship would no longer be a good one. I had no one to blame but myself though.

Shannon paused like she was gonna protest, but then she just went to her room like he'd asked. Mr. Breaux made sure she was gone, and then he turned his attention back to me.

"How are you, Kenzie?" he questioned and moved back so that his back was up against the back of the couch.

"I'm okay, how are you, Mr. Breaux?" I responded and nodded for some reason.

"I'm not doing too well, Kenzie. What happened with this other girl? Are you still seeing her or what?" He raised a brow and tucked his thick bottom lip into his mouth.

"No sir, I broke up with her before Shannon even found out about her," I replied promptly. I didn't want him thinking that I hadn't learned my lesson. Shit it had been months since Shannon and I broke up.

"So I'm confused as to what your intentions are with Shannon. I mean you seemed to be all about her, so this was a surprise to us all," he frowned and scratched the little bit of gray hair left on his head.

"I know, my own mother and father were pretty surprised as well. It was just a situation that could've been avoided early on, but I guess I was too much of a coward to take care of it," I said honestly.

My father was right in that I needed to stop trying to place the blame on Rosalind and anyone else I'd been trying to point the finger at. This was my problem, and nobody caused it but me.

"I see," he shook his head. "Now, what are your plans with my daughter? You didn't answer that part," he twisted his lips up and stared into my eyes.

"I plan to for one, never do what I did again. And two, I hope we can get back together and get married eventually," I smiled hoping he liked my answer.

"Married," he scoffed and sat up. "I mean, let's be honest here. You're pretty much for sure going to the NBA before you even make it to your sophomore year in college, we know that," he said and I nodded in agreement. "Do you really wanna be married knowing that you're going to the NBA, Kenzie? There will be women everywhere, throwing themselves at you all hours of the day. Do you honestly think you will have enough discipline in order to be faithful to my daughter?" he quizzed and clasped his hands together.

"I understand where you're coming from and I'm gonna be just fine, Mr. Breaux. My mama already gave me that talk and so did my father. At the end of the day, sleeping with these women who come after me isn't worth losing what I have with Shannon," I answered.

"Good. Well I hope you're able to practice what you preach, because if I ever see my daughter crying like that again until 4 and 5am in the morning, you and I are gonna have a lot of problems," he threatened. I could see in his eyes that he meant every word he said.

I wasn't scared that he was gonna do anything to me, because of the simple fact that he wasn't gonna do shit. I just nodded my head because I understood where he was coming from. Shannon was his baby and he didn't like seeing her hurt. But he didn't have to worry because she was in good hands now; she was always in good hands.

"Glad we could talk," he said and then got up to go get Shannon. I waited until her sweet perfume filled the air, and then I looked in the direction of the back and saw her beautiful ass standing there.

"Hi Shannon," I grinned.

"Hi," she replied shyly and gave me a small smile while nearing me.

I took her hand in mine, and led her out of the apartment as her dad watched us like Hawks. Hopefully this nigga found his chill soon, because when I got drafted and had to move, guess who was coming with me?

AFTER BEING SEATED, we placed our orders fairly quickly since we got the same thing all the time. I waited until the waiter left, and then reached across the table to take Shannon's hands in mine. I needed answers tonight, and they needed to be the ones I wanted to hear. I didn't know what I else I needed to do to prove to Shannon that I was sorry and that I loved her.

I made sure not to entertain any other women either during this break up, because my Auntie Nic said that would piss Shannon off even more. So I've been keeping to myself, and beating my dick when I needed to instead of sliding up in the many girls that offered me pussy. It was really bad when we played schools in other states, but I said I wouldn't be with anyone else but my shorty.

"I feel like I've been singing the same song for months, baby," I kissed the back of her hand.

"I know. I don't want you to have to keep apologizing and stuff. I just needed time to think," she said.

Thank God, because if I sent her another gift, a nigga may have to hit his dad for some cash. The school stipends only lasted for so long. I only got that shit because I played basketball, and they knew I couldn't get a job because of how time consuming the sport was.

"I know, are you still thinking? Or what's up?" I ducked a little to look into her face.

"No, I'm not thinking anymore. I realized that I do wanna be back with you," she said and then grinned widely.

"For real?" I beamed.

I felt like I'd just been told my jail sentence was over. I'd been waiting to hear those words for the longest, and at one point I was starting to think I'd never hear them.

"Yes for real, but no more chances, Kenzie," she responded.

"I swear I won't need any more. Baby you don't know how good it feels to hear you say that. I been missing you so much," I sighed and kissed her hands repeatedly.

"I know and I was missing you too. I thought I would've gotten over you, but every little thing reminded me of you and I thought about you all the time," she rubbed my hand. "No matter what I did, my love for you never died. Then when Kendrin got shot, I knew I needed to push my pride aside and follow my heart, because life is too short."

"You are so right about that," I nodded. I was thankful beyond belief that God had spared my cousin's life. "Give me a kiss," I bit my lip. She stood up and walked around the table to press her soft lips against mine. "I love you, man," I said in a low tone.

"How much?" she asked as she went and sat down in her seat.

"A whole fucking lot," I bucked my eyes and she laughed.

"Well, can you show me how much tonight?" she raised a brow.

"I can definitely show you tonight," I licked my lips as I thought about all the things I was gonna do to her. It'd been a long ass time since I felt her in that way.

TWO WEEKS LATER...

"SEE YOU LATER, BABY," I smiled up into Kenzie's face before he kissed me gently.

I watched him walk off to class as I stood in the doorway of mine. I loved him so much and I just knew that this go round was gonna be right. No more secrets, lies, nor bullshit to get in our way; basically no more Rosalind. For the first time in a long time, I just felt good overall. Nothing was wrong in my life, and I wanted it to stay that way.

"Hey," I heard a deep voice call out to me. I looked to my left and saw Christian standing there.

"Oh hey," I responded and looked up at him.

Before Kenzie and I made up, Christian and I were texting pretty heavily. There wasn't a day that went by that we didn't text until at least midnight. We planned to go out, but with all this shit going on we never got around to it; or *I* never got around to it. I kept having to cancel and shit, and just recently I'd stopped responding to his texts. And after every class for the past two weeks, I was damn near knocking people over to get out so he wouldn't be able to approach me. I slipped up this time though.

"How are you, Shannon?" he cocked his head.

"I'm good, Chris," I smiled nervously and hugged my books tightly.

"How are you?" I inquired although I really didn't care.

It was just awkward since I hadn't been responding to him. I was around Kenzie all the time again, and I didn't want him seeing me text another guy, so I couldn't exactly tell Christian to stop.

"I'm okay. I would be doing better if a certain someone would answer my text messages," he got close to my face as if he was gonna kiss me.

"Christian, I can't talk to you anymore in that way," I said in a low tone, as I made some space between us.

"What? What did I do?" he quizzed with furrowed eyebrows.

"Nothing, it's just I'm with someone now and he-"

"Oh, that basketball cat?" he raised a brow.

"Yes, that basketball cat. We're back together and-"

"I didn't think you were that type," he shook his head as he looked me up and down with a disgusted expression.

"What type?" I questioned with a frown.

"The type to take a nigga back after he dogged you out. You struck me as the strong type. The girl that knows her worth," he explained.

"I do know my worth, Christian. Just because I took Kenzie back does not mean I don't have any pride," I glared up at him.

"Oh, let me guess. You took him back because you loved him," he rolled his eyes and laughed at me. He was pissing me off, and really getting to me.

"Yes I love him and it's none of your business why I took him back. Look, I'm done with this conversation and I'm done with you!" I spat and turned to walk away. He grabbed me from behind, and pressed his hard dick up against my ass.

"You playing with the wrong one, Shannon. I always get what I want," he whispered into my ear and then kissed it. I snatched away and he laughed loudly before following me into class.

We both sat down, and all during class I would catch him staring at me and smiling. I didn't know what his fucking problem was. All we did was text, and now he was acting like we dated or something. I didn't have time for any crazy niggas, especially not when I had a boyfriend who had an even crazier fucking family.

Once class was over, I quickly grabbed my books and stuff so I could leave before him. As soon as I stepped out though, I felt his hand rub my hair, and when I looked back he was walking away with a smile. He blew me a kiss, and I power walked to the fucking parking lot on edge.

As soon as I got home, I dialed my friends on the phone and told them to come over. Willow couldn't, because she was helping Kendrin since he was finally able to come home, thank God, but Aysia and Gianna were over here in a jiffy.

Right when they came into my room, I shut the door for privacy even though my dad was at work.

"So what's the problem?" Gianna asked and rubbed her stomach.

"I think I fucked up," I said and paced the floor in front of them.

"Who did you fuck?" Aysia bucked her eyes and I smacked my lips at her. "What? I mean what else could it be?" she smiled.

"I think I woke a sleeping bear," I said and they both stared at me with confused expressions. "Okay, I met this guy, and we texted for a little bit because I was looking to get over Kenzie-"

"I thought you took Kenzie back?" Gianna frowned.

"This was before that!" I spat and she threw her hands up in mock surrender. "Anyway, that's all we did was text. But today when I told him we had to stop, he turned into the male version of Glenn Close," I ran off.

"Who the hell is Glenn Close?" Aysia turned her lip up and looked to Gianna who shrugged.

"From the movie *Fatal Attraction*!" I shouted and she and Gianna nodded to say they understood.

"So now he's stalking you?" Gianna quizzed with a confused expression still on her face.

"No, but he pretty much told me I fucked with the wrong nigga, as if he was gonna do something to me," I replied.

"Did you tell Kenzie?" Gianna questioned.

"No, I don't know if I should. I mean, he could've just been acting stupid. I don't want Kenzie trying to whoop his ass for nothing," I said. "He could lose everything if that shit hit the fan."

"But if you're this scared already, maybe you should," Gianna suggested.

"Yeah, this nigga got you pacing the floor," Aysia agreed.

"Maybe I should tell KJ," Gianna offered.

"No do not tell KJ!" Aysia and I shouted in unison. "You know KJ ain't all there, he'd shoot up that nigga's house," Aysia added and we all laughed.

"KJ is a last resort, Gigi," I smiled and she nodded. "Dammit. Okay, if he acts weird the next time I see him, I will tell Kenzie," I smiled.

"Yeah, I guess that's cool. Hopefully he doesn't kidnap your ass from class," Aysia joked and she and Gianna laughed heartily.

"Very funny bitches," I huffed.

"Let's go to Sonics," Aysia rubbed her small belly. We agreed and then gathered our things so we could go get something to eat.

I hoped Christian was just blowing smoke and not really trying to start some shit. I just wanted to have some peace for once. These past couple of months have been a storm for me, and now Christian was trying to bring it back now that the sun was finally shining.

THE NEXT DAY...

MY BROTHER GETTING shot was really bothering me. And on top of that, my dad was looking to me to handle it as soon as fucking possible before he had to. I had no problem with that, it's just I had no idea who the fuck it was. I was for damn sure gonna find out though, and boy was that nigga gonna be sorry.

I'd kept my ear to the streets for the past few weeks, and was starting to collect information here and there, but nothing of substance in my opinion. See, the difference between an actual thug and a wanna be thug was one simple thing: one was street smart and one was just dumb as hell. Most of the time niggas who try to come for people like my cousin, my brother, or myself are dumb niggas. These dumb niggas usually have some animosity towards us because they're jealous of our success. That success could be with women—shit, maybe we took their bitch. Or that success could be within the drug game. Most of the time it was the latter, but shit, niggas was bitches these days and stayed crying over pussy.

By saying that, I knew one would soon talk. This dumb nigga is gonna brag to his friends about how he shot up a King brother. I know he is. Because see a dumb ass nigga like him can't hold in the fact that they pulled a trigger. They're not a real thug, because a real thug has pulled a trigger plenty of times, and feels it's nothing to brag about. But see this wanna be gangster muthafucka was like a teenage boy getting his first taste of pussy, so he was gonna tell someone sooner or later.

I was gonna wait though, because right now that dumb nigga is trying to keep it a secret because he's scared; another reason he ain't a thug. But as soon as he feels the need to stick his chest out he's gon' be letting all his little homies know he put that bullet in Kendrin King. And guess what's gon' happen after that? One of his homeboys are gonna come back and tell one of my people, and that's for two reasons.

One reason is because that dumb nigga is too stupid to see he got some bitch ass niggas as his homies, who would snitch on his ass at any given moment to benefit themselves. And secondly, this snitch wants to be down with Kendrick King II. But what he doesn't realize is that after we collect this vital information, a bullet is gonna be put right between this snitch's eyes.

So like I said, for now I was gonna wait. And while I wait, my eyes will be watching every move the streets make. I'm gonna know about every conversation, and every little crime that goes down in Baltimore, whether it has something to do with me or not. I wanna know every dumb nigga there is, and I wanna make sure that no more dumb niggas attempt to prosper against me.

I polished off my glass of Hennessey, which I needed to calm myself down. I wanted to kill anything right now, but I needed to be patient and not become reckless, because that's how you slipped up and got yourself killed. I needed to get at the right nigga at the right time, but before he struck again.

I heard a knock at my office door, and I yelled for Gianna to come in.

"What are you doing?" she asked when she entered into my office.

She had on a little negligée, and although she had a belly, she was just as sexy as always. Her long brownish red hair was hanging down messily, and she had on the bracelet and ring that I'd given her.

"I'm thinking shorty, what's up?" I questioned before sipping my drink. She walked over to me, and stood between my legs.

"I miss you," she caressed my face before straddling my lap. Lately I'd been hitting the streets and then coming to my office, leaving her to sleep alone.

She leaned my head back and kissed me very gently as I set my glass down. We started to suck each other's lips, and then we let our tongues dance. I groped her body and ass, and then pulled her thong to the side from the back. I rubbed between her lower lips, and moaned at how wet she was already. She broke from our kiss, and reached down to unbuckle my pants and release my dick. Once it was out, she moved up a little, and then slowly sat down on the tip. Damn, she was so snug and soaking. I'd definitely been neglecting the pussy.

"Mmmm," she bit her lip as she sat there with the tip of my dick inside of her.

"Go down baby," I whispered.

She was feeling so good already. I'd never had sex with a pregnant girl before Gianna, but I was learning that pregnant pussy was fire as hell. I widened her legs a little, and she pushed herself down a bit more.

"Uuhh, uuuh," she whimpered softly.

"Keep going," I said in a low tone and kissed her soft full lips. I gripped her ass, and then pushed her all the way down, filling her up.

"Mmmm," she bit her lip once I was all the way in.

"Shit," I said. She was so fucking tight that I just had to sit in it for a few moments to gain my composure.

I rubbed up from her ass to her back, and then lifted her gown over her head to expose her half naked body; she still had panties on. I cupped her breasts and then licked her nipples as she sat paralyzed on my pole. I could feel her shit throbbing around my dick, and I could tell she was already about to cum.

Once I'd had enough of licking, sucking, and biting her nipples, I put her legs in the nook of my arms, and ripped the crotch of her panties. I gripped her small waist, and then guided her up and down my dick at a nice slow pace. Her pussy was strangling my dick, wet as hell, and boy was it pretty. I felt her long hair sweeping my knees as I moved her up and down on my rod.

"You're so sexy, baby," I bit my lip as I watched her make faces.

"Aaah, uuuh, Kendrick," she called out just as I saw my pole become coated with her juices.

"Damn," I whispered at the sight and the feeling. Seeing my dick slam into her, and her firm round titties bouncing, was so fucking beautiful in combination with her pretty face.

I gripped her waist tighter, and began to go ham. The sound of me plunging into her wetness was something I could listen to all day.

"Ooooh, aaah, aaah, aaah," she cried out and burst right then.

"Oh fuck, I'm about to nut," I grunted, and right after I was filling her up. She wound her hips on me a little, and it was so sexy. I slid out of her, and then she came closer to hug my neck.

"I love you so much, KJ, and I can't wait to bring your baby here," she said before sliding her tongue into my mouth.

CURRENTLY WE HAD a big ass problem. The three guys we chose to spray them Porn Star niggas missed a few of them. Now KJ and I had to go out and do the job ourselves, before these niggas went into hiding somewhere. And if they got away before we could catch them, it was gonna be some fucking hell to pay.

"I'm mad as a muthafucka right now!" KJ shouted.

"Nigga, me too," I shook my head, trying to remain calm.

Out of the three guys we'd asked to do the job, we killed two of them earlier. There was one more, but we would have to get him once we killed the rest of these Porn Star niggas.

"Talking about three of them ran too fast, get the fuck out of here," KJ shook his head and scoffed.

We were in his gunroom gathering up the weapons that we needed. This nigga had all types of guns, from shit that looked like it was used in the war, all the way down to little ass handguns. The room was guarded with two security codes, an eye scanner, and a big metal door.

"Damn nigga, why all these?" I chuckled as I scanned the wooden walls that held the one hundred something guns. I'm surprised this nigga didn't have a tank parked somewhere.

"Shit, you never know. I may have one hundred niggas coming for me, and if so, they won't catch me slipping," he responded and I nodded to say I understood while chuckling at his crazy ass.

For some reason, KJ was not scared of getting shot. He'd been like that since we were little kids. I remember one summer we would always walk to this liquor store, and there was this dude named Larry that used to always shoot people with his BB gun from afar, whenever people walk by. So one day during our daily trip, KJ spotted the nigga aiming his shit at him like he was gonna hit him. So KJ ran up on the nigga, daring him to shoot him, all the while getting the gun pressed into his chest. Larry kept the gun shoved into KJ's chest with his hand on the trigger, but he was too scared to shoot. From that day forward, I never saw Larry shooting his gun again. Keep in mind KJ was twelve, and Larry was about fourteen or some shit. I knew he was in high school for sure. I laughed to myself as I replayed KJ yelling, *Shoot me and I'm gon' rock yo ass! Shoot me!*

Once we were all loaded up, he threw me a duffle bag and then grabbed one himself. We exited the gun room out the side door which led to the garage, and then we got into an all-black 1981 Oldsmobile Cutlass with tinted windows. We threw our bags into the back, after taking out what we would need right away.

"Alright, so these niggas are over at those condos in Ellwood," KJ explained. "We're gonna go over there and just blast. They should be sitting outside around this time, so we gon' be on some drive by shit. Now when we hit the corner of Loney's Lane, they're gonna be right there. You drive and I will shoot," he laid it out for me.

"Alright, cool," I said and cranked the car.

As we drove, KJ loaded the gun and made sure everything was in place. Soon as we got ready to make a right on Loneys, I cut the headlights off.

"Turn them back on. Drive by once so we can check and make sure it's them, and then hook another right on Jefferson, then another on North East Avenue so we can come back around and blast them," KJ said and I nodded.

I drove by the area, and we spotted the three guys sitting on the porch smoking and drinking.

"Dumb asses," I commented and KJ laughed.

After making sure it was them, I kept going and made a right to come back around. I made the second right on North East, quickly made another on Pulaski highway, and then as soon as I made it back onto Loneys Lane, KJ rolled his window down just enough to stick his gun through. Right when we came close, I slowed down.

POP!

POP!

POP!

This nigga KJ hit each one between the eyes, and didn't hit shit else with just three bullets. I sped off and he slipped the gun back into the car.

"Should we make sure they're dead?" I quizzed.

"Did you see their heads explode like I did?" he grinned and so did I.

"Yeah, you right, that shit was crazy, nigga. How did you get your aim like that?" I asked as we sped back to his home in the Cutlass.

"My dad, nigga. I'm telling y'all he had me in some vigorous ass training before he gave me this shit," he responded and reached in the back for his duffle bag. "Aye, but let's pull up on Fish," he said. Fish was the head nigga we asked to spray these muthafuckas the first time.

"Alright," I replied and headed towards his crib. Once we arrived, KJ and I got out and rushed up Fish's porch steps.

"The back," KJ said.

We headed around the back, and climbed into his window. This nigga lived in the hood and had the nerve to have a broken window. Anyone could literally just crawl into his crib. I realized we were in an empty bedroom after I finished climbing in. I followed KJ out of the bedroom to the living room, where Fish was sitting up knocked out with cartoons on the screen.

"Aye little nigga, wake up," KJ whispered and lightly tapped Fish's face with his handgun.

He stirred a little, and then wiped his mouth to remove the drool. He looked around with his eyes low, and then quickly sat up once he recognized KJ and me.

"How you get in here? KJ, Kaleeini, what's up man?" he began to panic.

KJ just smiled and shot him in the face three fucking times. The sight was disgusting, but of course it didn't bother KJ's crazy ass. We made sure not to touch anything even though we wore gloves, as we waited for Blade and his cleaning crew to show up.

Once everything looked like it hadn't been touched, they bagged up Fish. KJ and I went and got back in the Cutlass, with him in the driver's seat this time, and then headed back to his home.

"I can't believe you woke his ass up and blasted his face," I chuckled.

"Bitch ass nigga," he chuckled as well and sparked a blunt as he made a left turn.

We got back to his home in about thirty minutes, put all our stuff away, and then burned anything that we needed to in the backyard.

I immediately took my ass home so I could shower and lay up with my girl. Once I finished scrubbing myself, I laid down next to Aysia. I kissed her stomach, which was starting to protrude even more now, and she woke up.

"I'm sorry for waking you," I whispered.

"It's okay," she half smiled and caressed my face.

"And it's all taken care of baby," I assured her, and then kissed her lips.

I reached down between her legs, and pulled on her panties by the crotch. A faint smile covered her face, because she was still half asleep. I got down between her legs, and placed her caramel thighs on my shoulders so I could eat.

"Mmmm," she cooed as she played with my dreads. I sucked on her clit gently, while massaging her smooth thighs. "Baby, aaah, aaah," she whimpered as I started to really get in there. "I-I'm gonna cuuumm," she screeched as she released into my mouth. That didn't stop me though, because I hadn't had enough. I kept sucking and flicking, and when I felt her try and pull away, I locked her waist down. She plopped back, giving up, and then exploded soon after. I licked her a couple more times, and stood up on my knees.

"Shit," I moaned once I felt her lips around my dick. She moved slowly, lubricating it, and once it had enough she sped up. "Aysia, fuck," I threw my head back as she massaged my balls. I loved that she didn't try to be cute with it, and it made her look even sexier anyway. "Aaahh, aahh," she had me calling out as I bumped her tonsils. I spilled my seeds down her throat, and then fell on my back.

She mounted my dick, and then slid her sexy ass down. She dug her nails into my chest at the feeling of me splitting her open damn near. I gripped her waist as tightly as I could without hurting the baby, and guided her up and down. Once she was good to go, she rocked her hips back and forth on me, making my knees weak.

"Do that shit, Aysia," I cheered her on and squeezed her ass.

"Oh, oh shit," she said as she released. She collapsed down on me, and I hugged her against my chest.

I began to hump upward, beating it up as she called out to the high heavens. I kissed on her neck as she caressed my dreads, while calling out. I pulled her face to mine so that I could kiss her, and continued to go ham between her legs until we both screamed out. Before we could even catch our breath, we kissed hungrily for what seemed like forever, as my dick rested inside her.

I was excited about today, because I would be finding out the sex of my baby. KJ was positive that it was a boy, but I felt in my heart that it was a girl. His crazy ass already had the nursery set up, and everything was blue. I felt so bad for him because he was gonna have to get it done all over in pink once we saw that we were having a beautiful little girl.

We sat in the waiting area of the doctor's office, and a smile was plastered across my face.

"What you over there cheesing for?" KJ questioned.

"I'm just thinking about your face when she tells us that we're having a girl," I chuckled.

"Shorty, I'm telling you now, my family only makes boys. Every now and then a girl slips up, but it's not often," he squeezed my exposed thigh. He was so sure of himself that it was hilarious.

"Well, just know that you're wrong, and that's all I'm gonna say," I giggled and kissed his cheek.

We waited for about ten minutes longer, and I almost fell asleep because KJ was rubbing my belly. Even though he was a thug, his hands were nice and gentle. I think it was because I made sure that he put lotion on his hands, elbows, knees, and feet at the least, every morning.

"King!" the nurse assistant called me.

We were using KJ's medical insurance that he put me on, and he put my last name as King. He was doing everything but getting his ass down on one fucking knee.

He stood up and helped me up as well, before we walked to the back with the nurse. She led us to a room, and KJ scooped me up to sit me on the bed.

"She thinks I'm your wife," I said.

"Good," he responded as he sent a text on his phone.

"But I'm not your wife," I raised a brow to see what he would say.

"You pretty much are," he stood up. "We live together, we have sex *all* the time, and now you're having my baby," he kissed my neck after listing each thing.

"I guess," I sighed and leaned back so he could stop kissing me.

For some reason, I felt like he was just blowing smoke up my ass. He wanted to play house but not have to be officially tied down in case he found something better. But if he thought he was gonna get me pregnant again before I signed some paperwork, he was sadly mistaken. I would be pulling my birth control out, and he would be strapping up if it came down to it.

"Good morning Mr. And Mrs. King, how are you?" Dr. Cleveland smiled at me. She was a short white lady with long blond hair.

"Good morning, and I'm fine," I exhaled still thinking about KJ being on his bullshit.

"That's great and what about you daddy?" She asked KJ, and for a second I almost snapped until I remembered she was referring to him becoming a father. I wouldn't be surprised if he fucked her before though.

"I'm better than ever," he grinned showing his deep dimples and perfect teeth. He was so annoying with his fine ass.

"Nice, so are we ready to see what's coming into the world in just some months?" She smiled and started to wash her hands. She was washing up her damn arms and everything.

"Yes we're ready, but I already know what it is," I chuckled as she helped me lie down flat.

"Oh yeah, what?" she inquired with a smile.

"It's a girl," I nodded because I was so sure.

"It's a boy. I tried to tell her I don't make girls," KJ shook his head at me with his lips pursed.

"Uh oh. I've heard men say that before, just to be crushed when they see it's a little girl growing in there," Dr. Cleveland told KJ, and I stuck my tongue out at him making him laugh.

"I feel bad for those cats, but I know how my body works," KJ tucked his lips in and sat back. I loved how cocky he was, even though he was wrong.

"Alright," Dr. Cleveland tittered.

She sat down on her stool, put on her gloves, and then spread the ultrasound jelly all over my stomach. It was so cold, but at least she was doing it slowly. Once it was spread to her liking, she cut the monitor on, and placed the camera thing on my stomach. She moved it around as KJ and I watched her on the edge of our seats. It was so quiet you could hear a mouse piss on cotton in here.

"Okay," she nodded and moved it around a little bit more. "Well, I guess Mr. King *does* know how his body works, because this is definitely a little boy," she grinned at us.

"Yes!" KJ shouted and clapped his stupid hands together. Dr. Cleveland laughed at his reaction, and so did I.

"He's a very healthy baby, and doing just great. Looks like you guys will have some very fat cheeks to kiss," she said and we chuckled. "Have you guys picked a name?" She asked as she wiped my belly off.

"Yes, Kendrick King III," I nodded and smiled at her.

"Ooh nice, I love to see a name get passed down. So many people these days don't make it past a Jr.," she shook her head and removed her gloves. She talked with us a little bit more about the baby, and then we were free to go.

"You hungry?" KJ asked as he cranked up the car.

"Yes, I want Miss Shirley's again," I responded happily. These days just the thought of food filled me with joy.

"Oh, and don't forget about our bet," he laughed loudly.

"KJ, I thought that was a joke!" I squealed.

"Nope and I already bought the shit I need," he said as he pulled out of the parking space.

We made a bet about the sex of the baby, and because he won that meant after I had the baby, he could tie me up in this little swing thing so he could have his way. I was so sure that this was a girl, otherwise I would've never agreed.

"I can't believe you bought it already," I chuckled.

"Yeah I did. It's the one where I can lock you in eight different positions," his eyes lit up like a kid on Christmas morning.

"I hate you," I pouted.

"You love me," he pumped the brakes and leaned over to kiss me. I cupped his face and we got into a little tongue-less making out. "It's gon' be another baby in there when I'm done with you," he cackled as he pulled from our kiss and sped off. *Nigga no it's not*, I thought.

Now THAT THOSE muthafuckas were taken care of, I no longer felt scared when I had to go out. I could finally leave Brice's bitch ass in the past, and damn it was about time. I hadn't seen him in a while for obvious reasons, but he had still been haunting me through his people.

For the first time in a long time, I felt really free and happy. I didn't feel like something was waiting in the trenches to tear my happiness away like usual. This was all thanks to my baby and my best friend, Kaleeini Drake King.

Whenever I would feel down he was always there to make things better, no matter what it was. Just like he said, it was his job to protect me and he was doing just that. To have a man that's willing to kill and lay anybody down for you is the greatest feeling in the world. I felt like with Kaleeini, no one could touch me ever. And now that I was bringing a baby into this world, it just made the love I had for him become stronger. I couldn't wait for us to be an official family. I smiled as I thought about my child.

I was in the bathtub with so many damn bubbles, that they were over flowing to the side. Willow let me have one of her bubble bars from Lush, and neglected to tell me not to use the whole thing at one time. So here I was in the tub, with bubbles sweeping my damn chin. I laughed at myself, as I continued to enjoy my hot bubble bath.

After I'd relaxed enough, I washed my body down and got out. I gave the full-length mirror a half smile once I spotted my stomach poking out way more than before. It wasn't as big as Gianna's obviously, but it was on its way.

"I can't wait to meet you. I don't know you yet, but I love you already," I said to my belly before wrapping a towel around my body.

"Aysia, what the fuck are you doing!" Kaleeini yelled through the bathroom door. I rolled my eyes at him. Here I was having a moment, and he had to ruin it. "I told you to take a shower Aysia, you better not be in no fucking bubble bath shorty!" he hollered and I laughed quietly. I was gonna take a shower, but I wanted to try the bubble bar.

"I did shower Kaleeini, calm down! I'm pregnant, I can't move that fast!" I responded still behind the door. I always used the *I'm pregnant* excuse whenever I got into trouble with him.

I grabbed some paper towels and wiped up the mountains of bubbles that had fallen off the side of the tub. Once I was done, I started brushing my teeth, and opened the bathroom door to see Kaleeini fuming on the edge of the bed.

"The reservation is for 8pm shorty, hurry up," he frowned and shook his head.

"Okay, you know I can't shower as quickly!" I turned my lip up after spitting the toothpaste out. I used some organic mouthwash, and then sauntered out. I wanted him to feel bad for rushing me.

"And since when do showers get bubbles in your hair with your lying ass," he flicked my shoulder.

I stopped to look in the mirror, and a bubble mountain was sitting on the side of my head. I just chuckled nervously and he rolled his eyes.

For tonight's festivities, I chose a simple dress that was burgundy and slightly short. I chose matching heels that weren't too high, and then slicked my hair into a low bun.

"Ready!" I beamed and Kaleeini shook his head.

I put my hand into his, and then we walked downstairs and out to the car.

We drove to B&O American Brasserie. I'd never been here before, but Kaleeini said it was really good. I knew it was gonna be an expensive place though, because he always took me to nice places. Once we got there, Kaleeini exited his car, and then came around to help me out.

"I forgot to tell your sneaky ass how pretty you look," he smirked and leaned down to peck me.

Kaleeini and I walked inside the restaurant hand in hand, and after letting them know we had a reservation, we waited for about five minutes to be seated.

It was a very interesting restaurant. It reminded me of a brunch held in 1930 or something. It was very clean though, and I was big on eating at clean restaurants. My tastes had become more upscale since being with Kaleeini.

"Nora will be your waitress tonight, and she will be over in just a few moments," the hostess told us and then walked away.

Nora came to the table in less than a minute, which I was very happy about. I was thirsty as hell, and I needed a drink immediately.

"Can I start you guys with some drinks?" she questioned while staring at Kaleeini.

"Can I get a glass of water, please," I smiled even though she wasn't paying me any attention.

"And I will have lemonade," Kaleeini told her.

"No problem, I will be right back with that," she floated away.

Nora was a basic white bitch with long dark hair, thin lips, and green eyes that were a couple shades lighter than Kaleeini's. She didn't even have ass or titties to make matters worse. I knew she wasn't on his level, so there was no need for me to get my panties in a bunch. I'm sure she was just a bored woman in her mid twenties, looking to get dicked down by a thug because she was tired of her little dick boyfriend at home.

"Someone has a crush on you," I rolled my eyes playfully.

"Who cares, as long as I only have eyes for you it doesn't matter," he shrugged and pulled my hands into his.

"Baby, you always know what to say," I stared into his dark green eyes.

"I'm just being honest," he said. "I wouldn't have attempted to get at you if I still wanted to play the field."

He was dressed in a quarter sleeve button up in blue, dark jeans, and had a chain that hung on his neck. His caramel complexion matched perfectly with his dark brown dreads that hung down sweeping his breastplate. My nigga was fine, so I couldn't blame Nora or any other bitch that had a set of eyes.

"I know. You don't seem like the player type. I used to think so before I met you though," I admitted.

"Trust me, I know. But I'm not here to play games. My dad told me a long time ago, that being able to be with one woman and not one hundred is what differentiates men from little ass boys," he explained.

"That is so true," I nodded. *Thank God for Kendreeis King*, I thought.

"Yeah, it is."

"I love you sooo much Kaleeini," I rubbed his soft but strong hands. "You better not ever try to leave me because I won't let you," I said.

"I won't because I'm sure you wouldn't let me. You're the type to be still trying to live with me and my new girl," he joked and I laughed.

"You know me so well baby," I continued to laugh and he shook his head with a smile.

Today, Willow and I were gonna go to the Circuit Court in La Plata so that we could get married. I was not playing around when I said that we needed to make things official.

When I got shot, I just knew that I was a dead man, and all I could think about was Willow. All I could think about was how I never got to make her my wife, and how badly I wanted to. I begged God to let me live, and that if he did that I would marry the girl that had been down for me and loved me with every bone in her body. Yeah Willow was bat shit crazy at times, but it was because she felt so strongly for me. She loved me so much that she refused to let someone try and take me from her. I would be worried if she didn't care as much. And the way she stayed with me in the hospital the whole time while I was out of commission, just further proved her dedication to me. There was no other girl that deserved to be my wife other than Willow, so why wait? It's not like getting married was the ending of my life, if anything it was just the beginning.

My mother insisted on coming, even though I told her a real wedding would still be taking place this summer. She didn't care though, she wanted to sit and watch. We did need a witness though, so I guess it all worked out.

"You ready, baby?" I asked Willow as she stood in front of her mirror.

She had on a pretty white dress that hugged her perfect body and showed her sexy legs that I loved so much.

I loved a fat ass and big tits too, but legs were my thing, and my shorty had the best ones. A bitch could be perfect everywhere else, but if them legs were foul I couldn't fuck with her. Them sexy legs led right up to that fire ass box, so it was perfect.

I slipped my hands around Willow's waist from behind, and squeezed her tightly.

"Yes, I'm ready now," she smiled and then turned around to face me. She grabbed my face, and stood on her tiptoes to kiss me.

"You're too short for that," I grinned.

"I'm average height, nigga, you're just tall as fuck," she smacked her lips with her ghetto ass.

I loved that shit too; that's how you knew the pussy was good. I picked her up so she could kiss me how she wanted, and then placed her back down so she could put her shoes on. Once she was ready to go, I called my mother to tell her to be on her way to the Clerk's Office.

We made it to Charles County in about an hour and a half. There were no closer places that could perform what we needed done, which was unfortunate, but it all worked out. I couldn't find one Justice of the Peace in Maryland though, so this was our best bet.

We went inside and my mother was fixing my collar and shit. I looked to her to tell her to chill out, and she had tears in her eyes.

"Ma, what are you crying for?" I chuckled as I stared down into her pretty face.

"Because I remember when you were just a little baby, and repeating everything KJ said," she laughed and so did Willow.

"Come on, Ma, not right now," I smiled.

"Oh my gosh. You had the fattest cheeks, and you let me kiss them as much as I wanted," she continued to reminisce as Willow grinned. "You didn't squirm and cry like KJ at that age," she rolled her eyes playfully.

"I was the cutest baby though, huh?" Kendria asked. I don't know why my mom let her grown ass come.

"Yes baby," my mother responded and Kendria was grinning widely as fuck.

We filled out some paperwork, and had to go through some extra stuff since neither of us were twenty-one yet, and then we were led to an office to get shit done. An hour later, it was official; Willow was now my wife and it felt good.

"When we get home I will start the name change process," Willow smiled. She was so happy now, and I loved to see her face light up like that.

"Can we go to dinner?" Kendria asked.

"I guess that's cool," I said.

"Nothing too much because we wanna have dinner with the whole family," my mom responded as we exited the building.

It was around twelve in the afternoon, and since I had yet to eat, Kendria's suggestion sounded like a good idea. We went to this restaurant named Texas Roadhouse on Dury Drive. It was a bomb ass steakhouse, and it had a nigga stuffed like a teddy bear. Afterward, we all headed back to Baltimore.

As soon as Willow and I got into the bedroom, we were ripping each other's clothes off. Once we were both naked as the day we were born, I laid on my back.

"Sit on my face shorty," I bit my lip at the thought of tasting her pussy.

She walked over to me, and straddled my lap. She kissed my lips gently, and then climbed up my body before lowering her pussy to my mouth. She gripped the headboard, and I gripped her ass cheeks before starting to suck on her clit.

"Oooh fuck," she whispered as I made love to her with my mouth. I was eating her pussy like it was the last time I would get to taste it.

"Kendrin, aaaah, aaahh," she cried out as she wound her hips onto my face. I fucked her with my tongue, and then brought it back up to flick over her clit. "Oh my gosh, fuck I'm gonna cum so hard baby," she whimpered and her body jerked lightly as she released. She was about to get up but I stopped her. I sucked on her pussy some more until she was hitting the headboard with her fist and damn near about to bite a hole into her bottom lip. "Baby pleaaasee, aaaah, aaah, oooh shit. Fuck," she purred and exploded again. I licked her clean, and she pulled away from me.

She got on the side of me, and then took my rod into her mouth. She deep throated it just the way I liked, and the sloppiness was perfect. You could hear my dick slipping in and out of her mouth all the way in Buttfuck, Idaho.

"Shit, suck it just like that, Lo," I gripped her hair.

I started to hump upward to fuck her face, and she didn't slow up once. It was such a sexy sight, causing me to burst so hard that I gripped her hair tightly in my fist. She swallowed up and then licked my dick once more.

"Get on fucking all fours with your nasty ass," I smiled and she giggled.

She got on all fours, and pressed the side of her face into the bed. Her nice round ass was in the air, and her beautiful pussy was on full display. I bent down to French kiss it from the back, and she started to cry out. Because it was sensitive, she came very quickly. I pushed my dick into her warm tight hole, and almost burst again on contact. I saw her ball up the comforter into her small hands as I plunged in and out of her slowly. Her ass jiggled every time I slammed into her, just the way I liked it to.

"Damn," I said in a low tone as the feeling of being inside her took over me.

"Oh, aaaah, aaah, aaaaah," she screamed and bit the comforter.

I spread her legs wider with my knees, and then started beating it out of the frame. She was calling out and twisting up her sexy ass face with every powerful stroke I delivered her ass.

"Whose pussy is this Willow?" I asked as I fucked the shit out of her.

"I-it's y-yours, aaaah I'm gonna cum so hard again Kendrin," she damn near sobbed and then gushed on my dick.

I slowed down so I could see all the nectar she produced, and then sped back up until I was filling her up with my soldiers. I pulled out and flipped her onto her back, before collapsing between her legs.

Today was one of the best days I'd ever had.

I WAS FINALLY LEAVING practice so that I could go home and nap before tonight's game. I wanted to be well rested so that I could put my best foot forward tonight. There were some scouts coming, and I wanted to make sure they liked what they saw. A part of me wanted to stay and finish college, but I knew I would get drafted before that could happen. I knew freshman year was the only thing I'd be able to complete, and I guess I was fine with that.

I'd seen plenty of guys go in freshman year, wanted by every damn NBA team there was, and instead of signing, they chose to stay and finish college thinking they could wait. But guess what happened? A faster, better player came into the picture, making that once good player a thing of the past. I was not gonna let that shit happen to me. Maybe if I weren't so heavily sought after by countless NBA teams, I would definitely look into finishing, but that wasn't the case so I had to do what I had to do.

As I was walking out of the gym, fantasizing about an ice bath, some dude bumped into me.

"Kenzie King," he smirked at me instead of saying excuse me.

"Watch where you going my nigga," was all I said as I kept walking. I was sore as fuck and didn't need anybody bumping into me. On top of that, he had the nerve to not acknowledge his clumsiness.

"You know Shannon is a great girl," he called after me, causing me to stop in my tracks.

"Fuck you say?" I spun around on my heels and walked back over to him.

"Shannon, your girl, she's very sweet," he chuckled.

"Keep my girl's name out ya mouth aight?" I hissed. I was not in the mood for this shit, nor was I feeling well, but I would still go toe to toe with his ass.

"Or what Mr. First Round Pick? What you gon' do? Dribble my ass to death?" He clapped his hands together, laughing like he was the new age Richard Pryor or something.

"You don't worry about what the fuck I'm gon' do, just know you don't wanna find out," I threatened.

"Hey, it's not my fault she came to me when y'all were having problems," he backed away with his hands up.

"What?" I furrowed my brows and looked him up and down. He'd better be just talking out of his ass, because Shannon knew better.

"Oh, she didn't tell you? Yeah we had a little thing going on before she lowered her standards and took you back," he chuckled.

I shoved him back hard as fuck, and he stumbled to the ground. He hopped up to charge me but my coach popped up out of nowhere and stopped him.

"Kenzie, go home!" he shouted to me. "Are you out of your fucking mind!" He added.

"Don't mention my girl again you bitch!" I hollered at old boy as he stared me down with eyes full of fire.

I didn't know who the fuck he was and what the fuck he was talking about, but he had me hot. Just the thought of Shannon having some little side nigga that she was venting to had me boiling like hot water. That's the ultimate no no. You never vent to the opposite sex about your relationship problems, because as a wise man once said, *a shoulder to lean on, soon becomes a dick to sit on.*

I threw my bag into my car, and watched as that bitch ass nigga walked off. *So that's why she wasn't trying to fuck with me*, I thought to myself. If she fucked this nigga we were gon' have some problems taller than the Empire State Building.

I cranked my car up, and then took a few a seconds to calm myself down. I didn't wanna be driving while I was angry, because that's how accidents happened. Once I was able to convince myself that he was just some hating ass nigga trying to get in my head, and that Shannon would never entertain another nigga, I was good to go.

I drove home, and when I got there, I immediately filled up the Jacuzzi tub in my bathroom with ice. Once I was finished filling it to my liking, I submerged myself in it. Not even a few minutes in, my mind began to imagine all kinds of scenarios about Shannon and this nigga.

Was she really talking to him and telling him about our problems? I hoped not because that would piss me the fuck off. And if she did really talk to him, had she even cut that shit off? She must've, because that's the only reason that nigga would've approached me like he did.

After sitting in ice for about half an hour, I turned on the hot shower to clean myself and melt the ice down. As soon as I got out, my mother was knocking on my bedroom door to bring me some food.

"Thanks ma," I smiled and kissed her cheek.

I scarfed down my food, set my alarm, and then took a little nap. I needed to get my mind on the game and off Shannon and that fuck nigga.

I WALKED into the gym and saw my teammates shooting balls around the court. As soon as my coach saw me, he waved me over to him.

"Sup?" I sighed and set my duffel bag down.

"What was that about earlier today?" he folded his arms.

Coach Johnson was a tall skinny guy with a huge ass belly. His hair was a salt and pepper color, and so was his thick mustache. I couldn't understand for the life of me, why a man with such a huge midsection felt the need to tuck his polo shirts into his pants. It only accentuated the gut.

He was a former high school basketball star, but during one of his games in senior year he had a heart attack. It was unheard of for someone his age to have a heart attack, especially because he was in such good shape. His doctor told him he either had to quit basketball or die, so he chose the former. Now he just sat down and yelled at us all day, which I guess was much easier on his heart.

"Man, that dude disrespected me," I finally responded.

"King, you have a lot to lose by fighting and shit. I know it's hard to refrain from whooping a couple asses, but if you want to see your last name on an NBA jersey, you're gonna have to," he explained and I nodded.

"I got you coach," I replied and he patted my back.

He was right, I needed to focus on my goals and not little petty arguments and shit. The last thing I needed to be doing was beating niggas up and catching cases before such an important game.

As we warmed up, people started piling in, and I spotted my mom, dad, little sisters, Kennedy, Shannon, and her friends. Kennedy was my half-sister because we had the same dad but different mothers. Her mom Adrienne died shortly after we were born, from a drug overdose. Kennedy recognized my mother as her own since she'd taken care of her from damn near birth. She had no interest in learning of her biological mother and her family. She looked nothing like her mom either, so it all worked out.

Shannon smiled at me, and I gave her a small smile back, but she was too far away to notice that I was slightly angry with her. She lifted up a big ass sign that she and her friends had created, and I couldn't help but chuckle at her. I loved how she was always my biggest fan. She put the sign down and then blew me a kiss, making my teammate Tyriq nudge me.

"Shut up, man," I laughed at him as we started to remove our windbreaker suits.

"She ain't got no friends I could get at? Shan is a winner, homie," he said as we continued to dress down.

"Nah, all her friends are taken," I chuckled and he sucked his teeth. I smirked at him, and then we took our seats to wait to be announced as a part of the starting lineup.

"Alright, are we ready to get this game started?" the announcer hollered and everyone in the gym roared.

There were so many people here it was crazy. Tonight we were going up against the University of Virginia, and I couldn't wait to show my ass on these niggas.

"Alright, from Saul High School in Philadelphia, starting point guard standing at 6'6, wearing the number two, Tyriq Renniiissss!" the announcer shouted as people screamed for Tyriq. He ran out onto the court, and waved to a couple people.

"He's been called one of the greatest new college players to grace the scene, and I'm sure you agree. From Forest Park High School here in Baltimore, starting shooting guard standing at 6'5, wearing the number four, Kenziiiie Kiiinnggg!"

I stood up and ran out as the crowd screamed so loud I thought my ears were gonna bleed. I looked at my people and saw everybody cheesing like Cheshire cats as I waved.

Once the announcer introduced the rest of the starting five, we got into the game. I had completely removed that situation with old boy and Shannon from my head, and was ready to show these scouts why they called me the greatest.

We won the game, thanks to ya boy, and I was ecstatic. Scouts from the Knicks, Nets, Celtics, Wizards, and 76'ers were all here, and had spoken to my parents and Coach. They wanted to meet with me, and that information had a nigga feeling good.

Once I got the good news, I quickly hurried to the back so I could get my shit together and see Shannon. After hugging my family and Shannon's friends, I pulled my shorty to the side.

"Great job, baby! You looked so good out there! The three-pointer king!" Shannon beamed and nudged me.

"Thanks, shorty," I half smiled.

"So I saw a bunch of teams talking to your mom, dad, and the coach baby!" she squealed and hugged my torso.

"I know, it's like all my hard work is finally paying off," I smiled down at her.

"Who would you pick?" she inquired.

"I don't know. I guess whoever is offering me the best contract. I'm eyeing the 76'ers though," I responded with a half-smile, and she nodded and poked her lips out for a kiss. I leaned down and pecked her gently. "Look Shannon, were you talking to anybody else when we were apart?" I raised a brow and her facial expression changed.

"Uh yes, but, we only texted and nothing else, Kenzie," she explained as I exhaled heavily.

"Did you tell that nigga about us?" I frowned down at her.

"I only said that we broke up because you weren't faithful but nothing more," she whined.

"Shannon, do not do no shit like that again! You know this nigga approached me talking about how sweet you are and shit? You better not have let him fuck!" I grimaced.

"Kenzie, I didn't," she shook her head. "I'm sorry, baby, and it won't happen again, okay?" she rubbed my arm.

"It better not. I almost whooped his ass," I said and she chuckled.

"Kiss me," she leaned her head back. I pulled her close, squeezed her ass, and pressed my lips against hers.

"What was his name?" I inquired.

"Christian Adams."

If I saw that nigga again I was gonna try my hardest not to fuck him up, because I would be pissed if he ruined my chances of going pro.

MY FRIENDS WANTED to take me out so we could celebrate Kendrin's and my union. It felt so good to be his wife, but I still wanted my damn wedding. The caterer and the bakers were still booked, as well as the venue and everything else I'd taken care of already.

This wedding so far was costing Kendrin a pretty penny, but he wasn't tripping about it at all. I was actually trying to go easy on his pockets, but I guess that wasn't working out too well.

I pulled up to the Cheesecake Factory, and parked next to Gianna's fresh ass BMW. It was crazy that she and Aysia now got to experience what it was like to be with a boss nigga; well officially in Gianna's case. Kendrin bought me a Porsche about six months after getting together, and I remember how in awe the two were. Now it was nothing to them because they got the same treatment. Shannon would understand too, just as soon as Kenzie signed that multi-million dollar contract.

I walked in and let the hostess know that my party was already here, and after giving her the correct name, she led me to the table.

Shannon, Aysia, and Gianna all stood up to hug me tightly, and smiles were plastered on everyone's faces.

"So, do you feel different?" Gianna questioned.

"Umm, not really. I don't think it has kicked in yet. Probably after the big wedding it will," I responded.

"And don't worry, I will be in full on workout mode after I have my son," Gianna said. I chuckled because in the past she was so sure she was having a girl.

"Thank you, boo," I said.

"Well, I will be fat as fuck at your wedding unfortunately," Aysia pouted.

"But it's for good reason," I laughed at her ass.

We ordered some buffalo blasts for an appetizer, and some strawberry lemonades. As we were indulging in the bomb ass buffalo chicken, some girl approached our table. We paused and looked up at her, and I waited to see if anyone recognized her.

"Can we help you?" Shannon questioned.

She was brown skinned and had a regular body. It wasn't anything special, but her boobs were huge. Her hair was long as hell, and either it was natural, or she had a really good weave. I could smell her strong ass body butter from Bath and Body Works, and it made my head hurt.

"Which one of you is Gigi?" She countered.

"Why?" Gianna quizzed. We weren't gonna get anywhere if people kept asking questions.

"Because she's fucking with the boss and I need her help," she responded and folded her arms.

"What kind of help?" Gianna questioned further.

"You must be Gigi," she smiled and sat in the empty seat of our table. *What the fuck*, I thought.

"Look, I'm trying to get hired at Kingin'," she smiled at Gianna and then crossed her legs.

"I'm sure you need to apply or something," Gianna chuckled nervously.

"Yeah, but I don't wanna do all that. I wanna have a shoe in, and I figured what better way than through his baby mama," she looked down at Gianna's belly.

"I mean, I guess I could talk to him," Gianna looked around the table at us and we shrugged.

"What's your name?" I inquired.

"I'm Shalyssa," she smiled and stuck her hand out to shake all of ours.

"Shalyssa, do you have a resume or anything that I can give to him?" Gianna asked her.

"Of course girl, I'm always prepared," she grinned and reached in her bag for the papers.

"Here is everything," she said as she handed it to Gianna.

"Oh, so you're looking to be a waitress?" Gianna frowned as she scanned the paper.

"Exactly girl, specifically in VIP where the ballers be at," she laughed and we gave her a fake one back.

"Well okay, Shalyssa, I will give him this," Gianna nodded with a smile.

"Ooh, thank you, girl. I was scared you were gonna shoot a bitch down. Lord knows I need this job, and hopefully one night I find me a husband in the VIP," she chuckled.

"As long as his last name isn't King," Aysia fake smiled.

"Oh no, never. I'm more of the basketball wife type," she responded and smacked her lips playfully.

"Again, as long as his last name ain't King," Shannon chimed in referring to Kenzie. Old girl was confused but she just laughed anyway.

"Well, nice meeting you ladies, and I hope to hear back about a job," she hopped up and jogged off.

"That was weird as fuck," Shannon turned her lip up.

"Right?" I shook my head and ate some more chicken.

"I ain't giving KJ shit," Gianna said making us cackle.

"You're not? Damn you gamed old girl up good," I laughed.

"Yeah, you were giving her the sweet Gigi and not the little sneaky one," Aysia said.

"Yep, I don't know what the fuck she thinks this is. She probably wants to suck his dick and that ain't gon' happen," Gianna smacked her lips.

"I wasn't even thinking like that. I thought she was just a thirsty bitch for a rich nigga," Shannon shrugged with a smile.

"Yes, and that rich nigga she thirsty for is Kendrick King Jr.," Gianna leaned in and poked her lips out.

She then looked around to make sure Shalyssa was gone, and then ripped her resume up. We snickered at her crazy ass, and then changed the topic of conversation.

"So remember that guy I told you guys about?" Shannon looked around the table, but I was confused.

"Oh, Willow wasn't there," Aysia said as she bit into one of the buffalo blasts.

"What guy?" I folded my arms after sipping my lemonade.

Last I saw, Shannon and Kenzie were back to being Noah and Allie from *The Notebook*, so I was perplexed to hear about some guy.

"Anyway, while Kenzie and I were on that little hiatus, I started texting another guy. Now, it was nothing more than texting, aight?" she looked into my eyes and I twisted my lips up. "For real, Lo!" she banged on the table lightly and I chuckled.

"Aight, continue," I said.

"So anyway, I told old boy that Kenzie and I had made up, and he got upset and threatened me," she shook her head.

"Did you tell Kenzie?" I quizzed as Gianna shook her head at Shannon.

"They told me to but I didn't. Anyway, why did this nigga approach Kenzie talking about how sweet I was!" she cocked her head.

"Sweet like as in your personality? Or?" Aysia raised a brow.

"Shit, I don't know. But as weird as this nigga is acting, he was probably talking about my box," Shannon scoffed.

"He ate you out?" I bucked my eyes.

"Bitch, I already said all we did was text," she chuckled at me along with Aysia and Gianna.

"So now what? You got busted, so you gon' press his ass about stepping to your man?" Gianna asked.

"I hadn't planned to. I was gonna ignore him, but now I'm thinking I should step to him because he's doing too fucking much," Shannon responded.

"Handle that," I said as the waitress approached our table to take our entree order.

After being out for about three hours just eating, laughing, and talking, we all parted ways and went home.

As soon as I walked into the bedroom, I heard the shower going. I stripped out of my clothes, and rushed into the bathroom to join my husband. I opened the glass door, and as soon as he saw me, he pulled me close for a passionate kiss. Being Mrs. King was the life.

THE NEXT AFTERNOON...

CHRISTIAN HADN'T SAID anything to me since that first time, so I assumed everything was cool. That was until Kenzie let me know that he approached him. I tried to just shrug it off, but I was pissed as hell at Christian.

The reason I was really pissed was because I didn't understand what the fuck his angle was. I did nothing but text this guy, and now he was going out of his mind! I could only imagine if I fucked him, or shit even kissed his looney ass. What was his point in approaching Kenzie? I mean did he think that if he broke Kenzie and I up that I would be with him? I hoped not, because that couldn't be further from the fucking truth.

As the teacher yapped on, I looked in Christian's direction out the corner of my eye. *Bitch ass nigga*, I thought. I scribbled on my paper in front of me because I couldn't concentrate on what the teacher was saying. I wanted this class to be over so I could curse his ass out. I had to throw my nice personality to the back for now, so that I could let this nigga know I meant fucking business.

Class was over ten minutes later, and I waited outside in the hall for his ass to come out. When he did, he had his arm draped around some bitch trying to lay his game down.

"Christian can I talk to you for a moment?" I raised a brow up at him. He paused, smiled, and then kissed the girl on the lips.

"Give me a few minutes, shorty," he said before smacking her on the ass.

"Okay," she giggled and then skated off somewhere.

"What's up? That nigga cheated on you again?" He cocked his head and laughed.

"Look why did you approach him with some bullshit?" I gritted.

"With some bullshit? I don't think it was bullshit shorty. I just told him the truth," he shrugged.

"Oh? And what's the truth?" I asked him with a frown.

"That you were feeling down and lonely, so you came running to me," he bit his lip and trailed his pointing finger down my exposed shoulder.

"Stop Chris," I moved my shoulder away from him. "And you're making it sound like I came to you for some dick or something. Actually, you approached me, remember?" I seethed.

"So, I saw the look in your eyes when you talked to me. You wanted this big dick all in them guts," he cuffed his crotch.

"Nigga, please. All I want from you is to leave my nigga and me alone. You clearly have a woman now, so just stop with the bullshit," I put my hand up.

"I'll do whatever the fuck I want, you don't tell me what to do Shannon," he smirked like a little sneaky child.

"You're fucking with the wrong ones, Christian," I warned him.

"I'm so scared of you and that fake ass Kobe," he scoffed and then walked away before I could respond. *He's harmless*, I said to myself.

I made my way to the parking lot, and there was a rose with a card attached to it. I opened my car, threw my books in, and snatched the rose with the card. *Look to your left*, it read. I looked to my left and saw Kenzie standing by his truck. I locked my car and then jogged over to him. I jumped into his arms and kissed his lips hungrily.

"You don't have practice?" I quizzed.

"Not for thirty more minutes," he raised both brows and bit his bottom lip.

"Here in the parking lot, Kenzie?" I turned my lip up and looked around.

"Yes here," he said and opened the backseat door.

"I thought you said no sex before practice," I grinned at his freaky ass.

"I said not before *games*. Practice, I can have weak legs for a bit. It's cool," he explained and licked his lips.

I climbed in and he followed me. I had a dress on, so he kept me bent over, and yanked my panties down my thighs.

"I'm about to bust before I even get my shit out," he joked and I laughed. I spread my legs a little more, and then I felt the pressure of his thick head at my opening. "You know better than to tense up, relax that shit," Kenzie demanded.

I relaxed my body, and he pushed himself inside me. It felt so good even though slightly painful. He pushed my dress further up my back, and began to pound me at the perfect pace.

"Oooh, ooh, aaaah, aaahh, Kenzie, baby," I cried out as he hit my spot with every stroke.

The way Kenzie dicked me down should've been illegal. He spanked my ass making me call out and bite my lip.

"Shan, this pussy man," he whispered as he sped up. I was scared that you could hear him tearing my shit up outside the car, but it was feeling too good for me to care.

"Uuuuhggghhhh!" we both grunted as we came. I loved fucking him in places that we may get caught at.

He bent down and kissed all over the nape of my neck, with his dick still inside me. My eyes were closed as I enjoyed the feeling, and allowed my body to come back from such a powerful orgasm.

When I opened them, I saw Christian watching us from a few

cars down. The windows were tinted so I was sure he couldn't see, but he was smiling like he could. He was staring straight into my eyes through the backseat window, sneering like he always did. He threw the cigarette in his hand on the ground, and then walked off.

"These windows are tinted, right?" I asked Kenzie as I nudged him off of me, making him slide his dick out. I knew they were but it damn sure looked like Christian could see us with the way his face looked.

"Yes shorty, you know that. Why?" he questioned and grabbed some baby wipes.

"Just making sure," I chuckled nervously.

Christian was really losing his fucking mind.

Once my brother recuperated, he started recounting all the events that night. I told you I was on a mission, and I felt like a damn detective. Nobody could get the information I needed quicker than me and right now I needed shit promptly.

Although a grown ass man, Kendrin was my little brother, and wasn't no nigga about to put some fire into him and get away with it. That went for any of my siblings, as well as my fucking cousins.

Anyway, as he explained everything to me that happened from beginning to end, it dawned on me; that nigga TJ was suspect as fuck. Why was he so hell-bent on trying to be a part of my operation, to the point where he felt the need to approach my brother after I'd already told him no? It just so happens that my brother gets shot a little bit after letting this nigga know that he couldn't help him? Nah, that wasn't no fucking coincidence at all.

I had my nigga Oscar look into this TJ nigga, and I found out some interesting things about him. Turns out TJ stands for Trenton James Jr. Trenton was the name of my father's best friend when he was younger. They fell out because Trenton and my cousin Kayden got into it over my mom's best friend Christy. He even went so far as to burst off into a hotel room and shoot Kayden ten fucking times over

Christy, and in the end my dad had to take his best friend's life. It doesn't stop there; no, it gets better. Trenton's mother, some old head stripper at King Brother's named July, was also murdered by my father, because she thought she could go against him to avenge her baby father's murder.

What was so ridiculous about that, was the fact that she was taking up for a nigga who died over another woman. What kind of shit is that? If Trenton Sr. had been worried about July instead of Christy, then maybe they'd both still be alive today.

Now that Trenton Jr. is older, I guess he felt the need to come for me, because he was probably too scared of my dad, or he wanted my father to feel the pain that he now feels for his parents. Shit maybe it was a bit of both, who knows. So here we are, dealing with this nigga because he's butt hurt over his two bitch ass parents. This sounded like some shit out of a fucking movie right now.

I wasn't just concluding all this off of putting two and two together either. Like I explained before, a dumb nigga had let the cat out of the bag, and that cat came right to me. TJ had someone else shoot my brother with his bitch ass. He got some rookie to the game ass nigga who had only used a gun to rob a liquor store. Word around town is that he met him the night of the shooting, and threw him some cash to do the job- dumb ass move. Never trust a nigga you just met with something so important, or you may end up dead, just like TJ was about to be.

Anyway, that rookie ass nigga started going around running his mouth about how he popped Kendrin King for TJ, just like I'd predicted he would. So not only was I able to connect the dots, I had cold hard evidence that TJ was behind Kendrin's shooting. Oh and that rookie's limbs are in a meat grinder at the moment.

Along with all that info, Oscar provided me the address that he was currently staying at on North Mount Street in Sandtown. I knew this nigga had no idea about Baltimore, because if he did he sure and the fuck wouldn't be over there.

It was around 10pm, and I was ready to put a bullet in this nigga.

I already had Blade waiting for that clean up call, and everything else was in place as well. Kendrin wanted to tag along, but I needed him to be fully well and enjoy his new wife for right now. Plus, this was gonna be easy for a nigga like myself. I laughed at the thought, because I heard TJ felt I was small potatoes.

I made sure the safety was off my gun, and then crept across the street to the front steps of his condo style home. I ripped one of the boards off the damn window, and climbed right through. I looked around the place and it smelled of piss and old onions.

"What the fuck!" I yelled in a low tone.

I went upstairs and spotted him laid out in the bed with two bitches. I laughed to myself because I'm sure he had no idea he was about to die. At least he went out with a bang. I pulled my mask from my back pocket, and then neared the bed.

"Aye shorty, get up out of here before I have to kill you," I whispered to the light-skinned chick closest to me. She hopped up and opened her mouth to scream, but I slid my gun into it. "Don't say shit, and get the fuck out. If you scream I will blow your head open," I stated seriously, and she nodded as tears ran down her face.

I slid the gun out of her mouth, and she slowly climbed out of the bed, grabbed her dress and shoes, and then ran off. I walked around the bed, and grabbed the other girl by her hair.

"Aaah," she whimpered softly.

She was pretty as fuck and her body was off the chain. Her smooth dark skin was supple as hell, and seeing her naked body brought all kinds of thoughts into my head. My dick started to get hard, so I had to keep my mind on the goal at hand, because it would've been nothing for me to have her go downstairs and wait for me.

"Get your sexy ass up out of here and don't make a sound. If you do, I will kill you," I whispered into her ear. She nodded and then I let her hair go so she could get her little shorts and top off the floor.

When she walked by, I grabbed her ass because I couldn't help myself. Once she was gone, I locked the front door and came back to find that bitch ass nigga still sleeping soundly. I sat in the chair in his room, and waited a few minutes to see if he would wake up. A real nigga could feel when something wasn't right, even in his sleep. Just like black women could feel when their little headscarf was about to come off in the middle of the night.

I took a small bottle of Jack Daniels out of my pocket and downed half of it. I stood up, and then dumped the rest over TJ's head.

"Huh, the fuck?" He hopped up and looked around his bed for his bitch. He finally realized I was there, and hopped out the bed with his dick swinging.

"Cover yourself with that fucking sheet!" I barked and he hurriedly covered himself.

"Now, I know you shot my brother and I know why. You need to realize ya daddy was a bitch ass nigga and ya mama was a dirty hoe," I said to fuck with him. He panted heavily because he was angry, but he was too scared to quarrel with me. I laughed loudly and pushed my mask up.

"KJ," he whispered.

"That's right. I think it's really nice of you to try and avenge your parents' death, but like them you're gonna lose nigga," I shook my head at him and paced the room.

"Ju-just let me see Kennedy," he stuttered.

"Fuck you wanna see her for?"

"That's my cousin man, I just wanna see her," he wiped some of the Jack Daniels that was dripping from his face. "She's really my only family member outside of my granny."

"Nah, I don't think you deserve that," I said nonchalantly.

"Look man, you should understand how I feel! I grew up with no mother or father!" He screamed and started to cry. "Then you and your brother dissed me! I had to get at that nigga because-"

"Muthafucka, do I look like the type of nigga to have sympathy!" I roared. "Do I? I don't give a fuck about how you had to grow up! The only thing I care about is the fact that you shot my brother you bitch ass nigga!" I hollered. "I don't care about you, your pussy ass daddy, or your pole hugging mama, so miss me with the fucking details!" I added. "And stop that fucking sniffling!" I screamed so loud, that his phone jumped and slid onto the floor. He quickly tried to stop sniffling, but looking at his face was making me angrier. "Who you got working with you?" I asked and cocked my gun.

"Ju-just my girlfriend Shalyssa," he stammered and I shook my head and laughed.

"Damn, you just like your punk ass dad, huh?" I smiled. "You ratted out your own shorty," I pursed my lips and shook my head again. He opened his mouth to talk but I blew his head open with two shots.

I hit Blade up to let him know, and his people were in and out quickly. I went and got in my Cutlass, so I could go home to shower, get my dick sucked, and sleep like a fucking baby.

I WAS CHILLING on the couch with Aysia, when my phone started going off. I looked down to see KJ's named flashing across the screen, and I knew it must've been important because it was a little late at night.

"Hello?" I answered and sat up, even though Aysia was lying on me.

She was knocked out cold, so her head just dropped onto the back of the couch without her waking up.

"Nigga, somebody shot up the fucking trap on Garrison Avenue after they tried to rob it," KJ exclaimed.

"What the fuck? How do you know?" I questioned.

"Rozzie just called me, man," he exhaled.

Rozzie was one of the workers in one of the trap houses over in Park Heights, and that was the one that got shot up.

"Meet me at my crib in twenty minutes, Kendrin is already on his way," he said.

"Alright, fa'sho," I replied and then disconnected.

I looked over at my shorty knocked out with her mouth wide

open and laughed. I lifted her shirt and kissed her belly, before rubbing it gently. I pulled out my phone to text her that I was gone out to handle some business, so that when she woke up and began to call me she would see it.

I slipped into an all-black Nike jogging suit, and then some all black Jordan Retro 12's. I grabbed my keys, phones, and wallet, and then booked it out the door. I got to KJ's home in no time, and then pulled through the gates after he buzzed me in.

"So what's the word?" I quizzed as I walked into his office and closed the door behind me.

"So apparently some random niggas came up in there trying to rob the trap. They asked for the codes to shit, and when Rozzie and them wouldn't give it up they start busting caps in niggas. I have no idea who would do this shit," KJ explained.

"I know because that TJ nigga been dead for a month," I agreed.

"What about his girl Shalyssa?" Kendrin furrowed his eyebrows.

"You honestly think she could pull off such a thing?" I frowned. If shorty had niggas out here robbing traps, then she was a bigger deal than I thought.

"I don't put shit past nobody," Kendrin shrugged.

"Yeah, you right about that. Ever since London blew her brains out in front of me, I've realized anything is possible out here," KJ nodded.

"Should we get Oscar on this shit?" I asked.

"Oscar needs a name or a hint or some sort of information first, before he can start looking shit up," KJ said and stared down at his desk like he was thinking. "Okay, so unfortunately we're gonna have to take this hit as a loss. But what we *will* do is install a camera system. Hopefully, the same people will strike again, and we can catch their asses. It may not be for a while, just because they recently hit us already," KJ huffed and ran his hands over his face. "Only for a short while though, because I ain't tryna have that shit recording every damn thing and then get into the wrong hands," he added and stared off like he was changing his mind about the camera.

"How much bread did they get?" Kendrin asked.

"They didn't get any fucking bread because that shit was locked up, but they got some work which angers me more," he said and then a smile suddenly spread across his face.

"What?" I chuckled.

"Them niggas are for sure gonna be selling our shit, which will be a sure fire way to find out who it is. If we have to kill our way up that's perfectly fine," he grinned.

"Kill our way up?" Kendrin frowned.

"Yes. When we get word of the corner boy pushing similar product, we're gonna get at his ass and he's gonna lead us to his boss," KJ responded and I nodded to say I understood. "So what we need to do is have a couple people keep their ear to streets, mainly listening to the customers. Once word starts to get out about there being similar product sold, we will know where to start. There's gonna be a lot of bloodshed, but it'll teach these muthafuckas to know their place," he finished.

"I'm with that," I said.

"Alright, so Kendrin, hit up Drew so he can rally up some street soldiers to be our ears. Tell him don't get anyone new, just the same niggas we been fucking with. I don't know who this is that robbed us, and I don't know who they've put out in the streets to be secret informants or what not," KJ said and Kendrin shook his head yes.

"What about this Shalyssa bitch?" I turned my lip up.

"Oh I'm killing that hoe on sight, as soon as Oscar gets back to me on what she looks like. I don't give a fuck if it's broad daylight, I'm dropping that bitch as soon as I see her," he cackled and so did we. "And if anyone else on the team spots that hoe, y'all better do the same."

"My dad was saying you're crazy as fuck just like your daddy. The both of y'all actually," I said and shook my head.

"The apple don't fall far from the tree, and the apples that fall, don't fall too far from each other," Kendrin responded and we laughed.

My uncle Kendrick was crazy as hell, and his sons were no damn different. They're probably the only niggas I know that ain't scared to die over some shit. If you put an AK to their head, they'd still call you all kinds of bitches and anything else they wanted to. My uncle Kendrick used to always tell us when we were younger, *Don't let no nigga who sheds blood just like you do, pump fear into your heart. I don't care if he got a chopper against your temple, don't go out begging another man for your life*, and I guess his sons took that shit to heart.

The way I was feeling right now though, I was ready to off whoever felt the need to get at us. Muthafuckas better be on their toes because we were about to heat these fucking streets up like no other.

I NEEDED to get a lot of stuff from Target for the baby, outside of what I would get from my baby shower in gifts. I wanted to mainly get some diaper boxes, bottles, and bibs, because my mom said those were the things that babies ran through the quickest, and that you could never have enough of them. The last thing I wanted to be out of when it came to my baby was bottles and diapers.

I was able to get KJ to come with me, which I was happy about because he never wanted to be a part of this stuff. All I did was pout and pretend like I was gonna cry, and I got my way. I was gonna miss being pregnant, because it tugged at KJ's heart strings a lot. I knew once this baby was here, I was not gonna get my way as much.

"Get the basket," I told KJ as I pulled my list from my purse. He did what I asked, but was doing something on his phone as he pushed it slowly. "Kendrick!" I whined.

"Alright baby," he chuckled at me and put his phone into his pocket. "Aye I need some loving if you want me to move faster," he grinned with his gorgeous self.

I rolled my eyes, and then walked closer to kiss his soft lips. Once he started to suck on my lips, I tried to pull away but he held me there.

"KJ," I tried to nudge him off. He squeezed my butt and then let me go.

We headed to the baby aisle so that we could start getting the stuff I needed, and I was hungry as fuck so I wanted to get this over with fast. Getting some food and a foot rub sounded like heaven right about now.

As we walked down the diaper aisle I heard, "KJ!"

I looked to my left, and it was some girl in tight ass jeans and a tube top; something I couldn't wear at the moment.

"Oh what's up Sylvia," KJ responded wearing that stupid ass grin. He always flashed that smile letting me know he fucked before. She rushed over to him and wrapped her arms tightly around his neck and squeezed. He hugged her back and I was furious. "Sylvia this is my girl Gianna," he finally gestured towards me.

"Oh wow, and I see a baby is coming soon," she fake smiled down at my stomach, and I just nodded with a fake smile as well. "Girl good luck dropping the baby weight, I heard it's hard to do," she added and clenched her teeth together. I was a naturally small girl, and I highly doubted that I looked big. Stupid bitch.

"They say sex helps you lose it quicker, right baby?" I smiled up KJ.

"I can't wait to find out," he bit his lip as he looked down at me, but then quickly brought his attention back to Sylvia the brick house.

She rolled her eyes at our little flirtation, and then said, "So KJ, I haven't seen you in forever."

"Yeah, I been busy you know. Working, and got tied down and shit. And I thought you moved," he frowned. *Tied down? Why did he say it like that? Maybe I'm just tripping*, I thought.

"I see you've been very busy," she looked over her shoulder at me disapprovingly. "And yeah I moved down to Gainesville for a little while, but it wasn't for me," she shook her head and turned her lip up. Were they seriously having a full on conversation while I was standing here? Really KJ?

"Oh alright, well it's good to see you back in Baltimore," he nodded and smiled. *Oh it's good to see her huh?* I rolled my eyes.

His teeth were so perfect, his dimples were so deep in his toffee complexion, and his green eyes were so beautiful. I could tell both Sylvia and I were admiring his features during a few moments of silence.

"Yeah, I'm happy to be back. I think I got back too late though," she bit her lip and touched his exposed bicep.

He was wearing a sleeveless black muscle shirt that was tight around the stomach; accentuating his already pronounced six pack. He wore grey sweats, and his dick print was showing out.

If my baby wasn't in my body, I would be trying to knock this bitch out for touching my man.

"Nah, it wouldn't have mattered," he chuckled nervously and pulled me closer to him. He kissed my lips, but I just sat there and didn't reciprocate.

"I don't knooow," she sang and eyed him lustfully. I could see all in her eyes that she wanted to ride his dick *again.* "Well, I hope to see you around KJ, and nice meeting you Gianna," she gave me one of those finger waves and switched off. I nudged KJ off of me, and went back to looking at the diapers.

"Gigi, please don't tell me-"

"You better shut up, and that's all I'm gonna say," I growled.

"Baby, relax," he whispered to me and grabbed my face to kiss me.

"No, move," I frowned as tears started to form in my eyes. I was so tired of this shit. All these fucking bitches, it made my stomach hurt.

"Gigi," he grunted and continued to try and pull me into a hug and kiss me.

I was keeping him at bay good though. I could tell he didn't wanna be too rough with me because of the baby, and that's the only reason I was able to keep him off.

"Just please stop touching me," I sniffled, and he finally let me go after smacking his lips at me.

He didn't say anything and just helped me pick out some diaper boxes. After getting some bibs, bottles, and crib toys, I was finally ready to go home and eat.

"So you not gonna talk at all?" he asked as we walked towards the register. He kissed the side of my head and rubbed my aching back.

"You can go talk to that bitch if you wanna have a conversation. Since it was so good seeing her, maybe she can come over tonight and cook you some food because I damn sure ain't," I spat and put my list into my purse.

I was so bored with KJ and all these little random sluts that he knew. They were everywhere like ants, and I was always standing there like a dummy as he talked and shit like it was cool. I was feeling like he didn't see me as someone that important, like a wife, because if he did he would learn how to act when those hoes came around. Letting that girl rub all on his arm and shit. I rolled my eyes at the thought.

We checked out, and then went out to the car. I didn't bother helping his bitch ass put the bags up; I just got in the car and buckled in. He hopped in on the driver's side once he was done, and then he leaned over to kiss me but I mushed him back.

"You must be crazy," I laughed at his attempt out loud. He sighed and then buckled his seat belt before pulling out of the parking space.

When we got home, I left him to bring the shit in, and then laid down since my back was killing me. After a few moments, he walked into the room holding a sandwich. He closed the bedroom door, and bit into it as he stared at me somewhat angrily. I rolled my eyes and closed them so that I wouldn't have to see his handsome face.

I heard some movement, and opened my eyes to see he had finished his sandwich and was now approaching me. He took his shirt off to expose his chiseled body, and then sat down next to me.

"Gianna, I'm sorry for flirting with old girl like that. I wasn't trying to be disrespectful I was just being nice," he said.

"I-"

"But if you ever come at me like that again, I'm gon' choke your little ass up a wall, aight? You don't tell me to shut up ever again, and don't ever call yourself not talking to me. I'm your man and you're my woman and you know I love you more than any fucking thing shorty. I would die for you. You mean everything to me, not these bitches that I give a smile or two to. But just because I love you doesn't mean you can go around disrespecting me Gianna," he stated sternly. I was scared so I just nodded. "Take your clothes off," he demanded. I stood up slowly because of my belly, and then started undressing immediately. He stood up as well, and once I was naked, he removed my hair from its ponytail. He bent my head back and started to slowly suck on my lips before dipping his tongue into my mouth to kiss me nastily. "Lay on your side," he ordered.

I laid on my side in the bed, and waited as he removed his bottoms and socks. He got into the bed behind me, lifted my leg, and slid into me while sucking on the nape of my neck and shoulders.

"Aaaah, aaah," I whimpered at the feeling of him pushing his entire dick inside me.

He pumped me slowly, while still holding my leg up, and the feeling was euphoric. I gripped the sheets in my hand, and bit down on my lip as he worked himself in and out of me.

"I love you, girl, and nobody else," he whispered and sucked on my neck again.

"Mmmm," I grunted softly as I came on his dick. He was moving nice and slow in a circular motion, and it felt so good. In, out, in, out, with every move I felt my clit throb. He was fucking my soul right now and he wasn't even doing much. "Kendriiicckk," I cried out as he hit my spot repeatedly. He rammed me, and then slid himself out slowly. I trembled because it felt so good in combination with him kissing and sucking on my neck. "I love you baby," I purred as I released again on his rod.

"Damn," he commented as he wound his hips with every pump he gave.

"Oh shit," he said. I loved the sound of his voice, especially during sex. His moans were so sexy.

"Oooh, uuuh, uuuuh, uuuuh," I twisted my face and I didn't care how I looked.

"Shit," he said again in that tone that I loved so much.

He sped up just a little, but still wasn't going too fast, and finally we both exploded together. He let my leg go, and grabbed my breasts in his hands. He pulled me into his chest, and I turned my face around to kiss him as he rubbed my belly.

THIS AFTERNOON WAS Gianna's baby shower, and I was excited because she looked like she was gonna pop any minute now. I couldn't wait to see the baby, because I wondered who he was gonna look like. Gianna was beautiful, and KJ was obviously a looker, so the baby would be cute regardless. I just imagined a toffee colored little boy with green eyes, dimples, and fat cheeks.

I walked into the room where Gianna and KJ had everything set up, and it was so cute. The walls were blue with little yellow ducks all over it, and there was a table set up with a matching table cloth. There was a tray of cupcakes on it, and they were pushed together to look like a cake that had *K-Three* on it. The carpet looked just like the walls, and so did the chairs, plates, napkins, and cups. They really went all out for the King family's newest addition.

"What the hell? Are you guys gonna leave the room like this?" I questioned Gianna.

"Hell no. I told KJ that we didn't need to do all this permanent stuff but he insisted. He said we could use it for the next boy's baby shower," she rolled her eyes and I laughed.

"Already talking about baby number two before number one gets here," I said as the cheese and fruit plate caught my eye. I was pregnant myself and needed some snacks now.

"No he didn't mean right away. And like I told him, I need to be someone's wife before I have two babies," she sighed and placed my gift on the cute little table. "You know these niggas pump kids in one bitch, just to leave her for some other hoe with a childless body," she chuckled and so did I.

"Do you think he's ready for marriage?" I quizzed and she shook her head no.

"Not at all, and probably won't be for a while," she exhaled and then moved some things around on the table to make room.

She was wearing a tan dress that hugged her cute shape. Her belly wasn't that big although she was gonna have the baby soon. She wore matching sandals, and her long ass hair was in one braid down her back.

"Why did you say it like that?" I asked as I finally reached for one of the snacks.

"Because he still acts like he used to before we became boyfriend and girlfriend sometimes. Do you know the other day some whore came up to him smiling all in his face, and they had the nerve to converse and flirt while I stood there like an idiot. I felt like a waitress or some shit. I was ready to offer them a drink if I could find a place to make it," she turned her lip up as I burst into laughter.

"You know they do have Keurigs in Target," I joked and she giggled.

"I will keep that in mind if it happens again, because I don't wanna miss out on a good tip," she replied sarcastically and I chuckled.

"I think it's just the hormones Gigi," I said. "What did you want him to do? Ignore her?" I questioned still chuckling and eating crackers.

"No, but he could've toned down the smiling and the damn sparkle in his eyes," she was laughing herself by this time.

"This is so bomb!" I heard Willow's voice, and we turned to look at her walking into the room.

"Hey cuties," she beamed and gave Gianna and I a hug.

Ever since this bitch got hitched, she'd been on cloud nine. It was good to see her this happy, because she loved her some Kendrin King. I always felt like she loved him more than he loved her, but I was glad to see I was wrong.

"Who cooked for the shower?" she quizzed and squinted her eyes.

"I made some lasagna for everyone, but KJ's mother cooked everything else," Gianna smiled.

"Okay, good. What about Kaleeini's mom?" she nibbled on her bottom lip.

"Yes, we have Morgan's cinnamon buns," Gianna rolled her eyes playfully, as Willow clapped her hands together. "They're right here, but this tray is KJ's," Gianna lifted the foil on one. She then lifted the foil on another pan, and grabbed a piece of Nic's famous spicy fried chicken. She closed her eyes as she bit into the wing, and shook her head. "Seasoned so well," she commented and we snickered at her. I then grabbed one myself, because the shit was fire.

Shannon arrived a couple minutes later, as well as the grandparents Nic and Kendrick, Kaleeini and his parents Morgan and Kendreeis, Kenzie and his parents Jessica and Kendon, Drew and his parents Kendrew and Deija, and even Kayden King and Christy with their daughters, Kaylie and Kaylyn; just every damn body. Gianna's mom Fiammetta and her dad Gary were also in attendance, and they brought a nice amount of people too. It was so many of us and I really liked that.

My family was fairly small because my mother had no siblings at all. My grandparents had her in their fifties, and since she had me at thirty-two, they died before I was even born. My father was some young guy that my mom met and slept with on a whim. When she told him about me, he didn't want anything to do with the pregnancy, and told her to never reach out to him again. When she dropped by his house, she found out that he was only seventeen years old, and not twenty-five like he'd said. His mother threatened to call the police on her if she ever dropped by or contacted him again, so my mother just left it alone. No one knew the details about my father except for Kaleeini. Everyone else thought he was staying in Germany, and that we corresponded through letters and gifts. I guess I was just too embarrassed to tell them the truth, but I knew Kaleeini wouldn't judge. By saying that, all my life it'd just been my mom and I, and she did a great job taking care of me. But now that Kaleeini and I were bound by a baby, we could sort of share his family.

After everyone ate and stuffed themselves, Gianna and KJ opened gifts, and then everyone went and chilled in different rooms. KJ, Kaleeini, Drew, Kendrin, and Kenzie went to play video games, the parents went to the den, and all of the girls went to this room that KJ had created just for Gianna.

I don't know why she was so paranoid that this nigga didn't love her, because it was so obvious. Not only did she have this room to relax in, but she also had an office where she could study and create fashion. She even had a separate phone line to give out to people who wanted her to style their little photo shoots. All of that shit was courtesy of her nigga. Not to mention the cars, clothes, jewelry, and the constant posts on his Instagram about how beautiful she was and how much he loved her. I think she was just paranoid that a guy like KJ could only be that way for so long, but hey maybe I only saw the half of it.

"So when do you find out the sex of your baby, Aysia?" Kendria asked me.

"In two weeks. I didn't want to find out at first, but now that Gianna knows hers, I wanna know mine," I nodded.

"Oh, and what do you think it is?" Willow smiled.

"Whatever you do, don't make a bet on it," Gianna said.

"Why? What did you get yourself into?" I looked her way and she pretended to zip her lips as she sipped her apple cider.

"Gigi!" Shannon bucked her eyes at her.

"Fine. I bet KJ that if it was a boy, he could buy and use this little sex thing on me. You can basically lock the person in certain positions, and it comes with a swing too," she scoffed as we died laughing for what seemed like forever.

"Ugh, I did not need to hear that!" Kendria covered her ears but was still laughing with us.

"Oh my gosh, this bitch gon' be bowlegged for months!" Willow shouted making us laugh for longer.

"Poor Gianna," I said as I wiped the tears I'd produced from laughing so hard. Kaylie, Kaylen, and Kenzie's sisters Kendlie and Kennedy were cracking up too at poor little Gianna's expense.

"I can't even believe my brother has enough stroke," Kendria turned her lip up and looked at a laughing Kendlie.

"Girl, he got too much stroke, that's why we have this going here," Gianna caressed her cute round belly.

"Let me know if I need to tell my mom to get you a wheelchair, you know she works in the old folks' home," I taunted causing everyone to double over in laughter.

"KJ, the pussy crook," Willow added. "Nah, the pussy vandalist, because he about to tag that box!"

"Please, my fucking stomach hurts!" Shannon shouted as tears built up in her eyes from laughing so hard.

"I hate y'all hoes," Gianna chuckled and shook her head at us all.

"Well thanks to you, no bets will be made," I panted and sipped my cider.

"What would you have gotten if you won Gigi?" Willow quizzed.

"Breakfast in bed and nightly foot massages for a week, and a new Hermes bag," she responded.

"Bitch, what? Your ass should've lost. You could get that any day," Shannon shook her head.

"Just know, if you see me wheeling up to y'all asses, you will know why," Gianna cocked her head as we let out hearty laughs.

My brother scheduled a meeting for early this morning, so it must've been hella important. The call time was for 7am, and the only time he wanted us there super early or super late, is when it was some shit.

I figured he may have found out who robbed our trap house in Park Heights, but then again we hadn't heard anything from the streets. Clearly whomever robbed us had yet to try and push the shit. I knew they weren't doing it on the low, because the streets weren't that loyal to some nobody ass niggas. We controlled that shit and anytime we wanted information we got it. I knew as soon it hit that addict's nose, they would know it was our shit. I guess addicts were good for something other than getting high.

I slipped my arm from under Willow who was sleeping soundly. I wore her ass out last night, and wanted to again this morning, but I didn't have time. It was going on 6am, and the snooze button had already been hit three times.

I climbed out of the bed, and then went to the bathroom so I could brush my teeth and shower. Once I was all cleaned up, I slipped into some dark jeans, a gray t-shirt, a black Versace hoodie, and some white, gray, and black Jordan retro 3's. I adorned my wrist with my Cartier, and brushed my fresh fade. I was a handsome ass nigga for sure.

I kissed Willow on her cheek, and then dipped out to the warehouse. When I walked into the room, all the top people were there. This only happened when we had to possibly do a whole lot of killing, or some super strategic ass planning.

I dapped up my brother, Kaleeini, Drew, Lenny, Oscar, and Tesean, before sitting down next to my brother.

"Alright so," KJ started his sentence and then wiped over his face. "Oscar tell them about the storm you've predicted," KJ gestured towards Oscar who had his laptop out.

This nigga had a new laptop every time I saw him, at my brother's request of course. Any time we had him do some hardcore research, KJ would order him a new one and have the previous one burned.

"So I got word that these cats named Duck and Lucky are coming this way from Camden, NJ. They run shit out there and are trying to expand to the DMV area. Now these guys are pretty ruthless according to word of mouth, and they plan to come through and take over with ease," he explained making everyone's face twist up.

"Do these niggas know who run the DMV area?" Kaleeini quizzed with a frown, and Oscar nodded slowly with his eyes closed.

"Oh, they have definitely heard of the King brothers, and they don't see anyone as a threat. Just like you, these niggas are undefeated and have a strong team just like you as well," Oscar said. We did not need this right now, especially since we still had no idea who robbed the Garrison avenue trap house.

"So this ain't gon' be like with all them other people who have tried to come for us," KJ looked all of us in the eyes. "We gon' have to work harder and smarter, which means less time fucking ya bitch on the balcony, and more time making sure you have a gun and bulletproof everything. I refuse to lose against these niggas; I won't," KJ shook his head. "They'll have to put thirty bullets in me for me to stop, and I put that on everything I love," he added and I nodded in agreement.

"So do you have any idea on when they're coming?" Drew frowned.

"Nah I don't. I wish I did but that's all I have," Oscar responded. "My homie lives out in Collingswood, and he said that people been whispering through the streets about it. They been celebrating and everything already, that's how confident they are."

"Get me them niggas real names, because I know it ain't Duck and Lucky. I want their first, middle, last, and the same for any wives or baby mamas they may have if you can," KJ told Oscar.

"You got it boss. I should have that in about two days," he said.

"Make it one day," KJ stared at him and he nodded. KJ dismissed Oscar, and Bolo escorted him out. "Yo, please have a gun on you at all times, and a bulletproof vest if possible. If I lose any of you because of them, I may go insane. As for any girlfriends, fiancés, wives, or even fuck buddies that you may give a fuck or two about, please do what you can to keep them safe. Like Oscar said, he doesn't know when these niggas plan to show up. They sound like some cocky niggas, and it may work to our advantage," KJ explained.

"Because they have no idea what they're up against," I said.

"Exactly. Let them think they can just come through here and conquer our area, because they're gonna get a nice surprise," KJ nodded and grinned.

"I bet they're some older niggas who think their age and years in the game mean something," KJ's best friend Lenny scoffed.

"Oh I know they are, and I don't give a fuck. My last name is King so I never lose. My name rings bells from here all the way to South Central Los Angeles, so they better be prepared," KJ said and we all nodded in agreement. "Now tomorrow morning I want to meet at the gun house," he added.

My brother had a gun warehouse in Havre de Grace, right next to the Susquehanna River, where we've dumped a plenty of people's ashes. The gun warehouse was full of a variety of guns and knives, more than the ones he had at his house. I think he had them shipped from other countries, because some of them I knew were not at the local shops.

After chopping it up for a little bit longer, we parted ways. During the drive home, all I kept thinking about was how shit was about to get real. I'll be damned if I get shot up again though!

Tonight was Drew's nineteenth birthday, and he was having it at Kingin'. I was definitely in the mood to party, because this season we were undefeated in basketball, and I'd gotten some pretty solid ass offers. Not only that, I was just asked to do a couple college sports magazine covers and a Nike commercial. I was on my way up, and wasn't shit gonna stop me. So tonight, I just wanted to turn up with my family and my girl, and celebrate my life and my cousin's birthday.

I put my fitted cap on, and then grabbed my phone to see if my shorty had text me and let me know she was ready. I saw that she had, so I grabbed the keys to my truck and headed out. After picking Shannon up, we drove straight to Kingin' to begin the festivities.

As usual it was packed as hell outside. Most people were coming in to party and spend plenty of money on strippers and liquor, but some people were just hanging out hoping to get in for free. I hated the hoes that hung around the door wishing that the bouncer found them to be cute enough to get in without paying. KJ never wanted these hoes coming in free unless they were so fine that he planned to fuck. But now that he had Gianna, those chances were slim to none.

I dropped my keys into the valet guy's hand, and then locked arms with Shannon as we rolled to the front. Bolo was working the door, so he just nodded to say what's up, and pulled the rope out of our way. Inside, the music was loud as hell, and some bitches were already on stage doing the most. Currently there were two girls up there, and one was licking the other's nipple. Friday nights on the strip club floor always got wild as hell. I remember one time two bitches were damn near fingering each other on stage.

Each floor of the club was about 2,000 square feet, and every damn inch of each floor was covered with people, except for where the huge ass stage was of course. I knew KJ, Kaleeini, and Kendrin were balling out of fucking control just off this place alone, even though it was just to clean their drug money.

"Damn look at all that money!" Shannon pointed to stage where the girls were.

The floor of the stage was covered in so many bills, that you could get up there and swim. If you were to lie down, they could bury your ass with the money for sure.

"Why didn't I become a stripper again?" Shannon joked.

"Because that pussy is exclusive to my eyes only," I pulled her into my body as we passed a couple of rowdy ass niggas. If somebody bumped my shorty I may lose it, and I couldn't afford that right now.

"Oh yeah," she chuckled and kept her eyes on the chicks on the stage. "I guess niggas love fake lesbians," Shannon added.

"They do," I laughed and she pinched me.

We walked through all the tables of people sitting down and drinking, and then we strolled to the side where the flashy ass VIP booths were. I spotted Aysia sitting in Kaleeini's lap, so I knew we'd found the right section finally.

"Damn it's live as hell in here shorty," I said to Kaleeini. I dapped him up as he held onto Aysia with his other hand.

"I know, which means more money in my pocket," he laughed.

There were plenty of drinks laid out, and Drew's underage ass was already twisted with a blunt between his fingers. The only reason we could drink in here was because KJ owned the place. Any other underage muthafuckas could not get a drink.

I found myself a seat on one of the velvet couches, after wishing Drew a happy birthday. Shannon began dancing in my lap once "Wrist" by Chris Brown started playing, and I gripped her waist as I enjoyed the show. In the middle of her dancing, I saw KJ walk up into the VIP, and Gianna got up to hug him. He palmed her stomach, and then they started kissing like some freaks.

Them two didn't give a fuck where they were, they always kissed like they were about to start fucking. It's been a couple instances where I just knew they were about to have sex in front of all of us. I guess the fact that they hadn't even been together a damn year yet and were already having a baby, should've told us something. I laughed at my thoughts.

"A dance for the birthday boy?" This girl stopped by the VIP, and Kaleeini tapped Drew on the chest to snap his crossfaded ass back to reality.

"She wanna dance for you," Kaleeini chuckled, and Drew waved her up into the section. She started popping her ass in his lap, and he was smiling from ear to fucking ear.

A couple moments later, some waitress brought a cake and some food for everyone to enjoy, along with more virgin cocktails for Aysia and Gianna.

As Shannon and I were eating, I noticed that nigga Christian walk by. I wondered how the hell he was even able to get in here, because by this time it was $100 just to come inside. That $100 didn't even include one of the regular tables on the floor, nor any bottle service. You would literally have to stand after paying a whole $100. He was an idiot if he did that.

I ignored him and kept eating and enjoying myself with my cousins, until he walked his ass by again.

"Man this nigga," I scoffed just as KJ was making another plate for Gianna.

"Who?" He frowned.

"Whack ass nigga walking over there," I pointed to Christian who was mackin' on this one shorty that had her a table on the floor.

"What's up with him?" Kaleeini quizzed as KJ watched him.

"He's just been getting on my fucking nerves," I scoffed as Shannon rubbed my back. She looked a little nervous, and that shit pissed me off that he was making my girl feel uneasy.

"What's he been doing?" Kendrin asked as Willow stared with a worried expression. Willow knew her nigga was off kilter, and that's why they were a match made in heaven.

"Trying to pretend like he fucked Shannon and all this dumb bullshit," I responded and Kendrin nodded with his lips pursed.

He moved Willow from his lap, got up, and then he and KJ made eye contact before smiling. KJ quickly handed Gianna her plate, and when she asked where he was going he ignored her. KJ and Kendrin made their way to Christian, and when I saw them talking to him I hopped up to go see.

"Stay here," I told Shannon.

Kaleeini and Lenny stayed back to keep the girls calm. Drew was still in his own world with that stripper chick.

As I made my way through the crowd, I saw Kendrin pulling Christian towards the back by his shirt collar, as he hollered and flailed wildly. People were laughing loudly and calling Christian all kinds of names as he got dragged through the club like a bitch.

I caught up to them just as Christian was being hauled through the back door. Kendrin finally let him go, and he tried to get buck so KJ slammed him into the brick wall by his throat.

"Aye you got a problem or something little nigga?" KJ hissed as he pinned Christian to the wall by his neck. I swear my Uncle Kendrick and Aunt Nic had some crazy ass kids. Christian just panted heavily as he shot daggers at Kendrin for embarrassing him. "Oh you wanna fight my brother? Go ahead," KJ let Christian go, and I just shook my head because I knew Kendrin was gonna kick his ass. If I had to fight anybody, Kendrin would be the last person.

As soon as Christian ran up on him, Kendrin delivered a three piece that had this idiot dazed and confused than a muthafucka. After he stumbled and spun around a couple times looking like Bojangles, KJ shoved him into the wall again.

"The next time you feel the need to be funny and shit with my cousin and his girl, I'm gon' pull my .44 magnum Henry Big Boy out on you," KJ threatened him. He tried to nod but that blow Kendrin hit him with still had him out of it.

As soon as KJ let go of his neck, he slid to the floor and sat there like a kid in time out. I didn't think he could walk right until he got his head together.

"Save your hands and feet for the NBA," Kendrin tapped my shoulder as we all went back into the club from the back entrance. The club goers were acting like nothing happened as they continued to turn up.

"Y'all niggas are crazy," I chuckled as we made our way back into the VIP and sat back down.

"Thank you for your kind words," KJ placed his hand over his heart, and we all laughed as Kaleeini and Lenny smiled widely.

For the rest of the night we enjoyed ourselves, and when we left, Christian was knocked out sleep in the back parking lot. Shannon and her friends made sure to take pictures.

"Oh my gosh Willow, what the fuck!" Gianna shouted as she, Aysia, and Shannon laughed.

Willow had squatted down and took a selfie with that nigga while he was knocked out on the ground.

"Don't post that shit," Kendrin chuckled as he helped his wife up off the ground and kissed her.

"I won't daddy, this is just for my personal pleasure," she responded making us laugh, as we exited the back parking lot.

GIANNA and I were at the mall because we wanted to shop, and because she said her doctor told her that walking would make the baby come faster. I guess she was ready to get him out of her. I was gonna miss her being pregnant, because she was too cute.

"I cannot wait to be able to wear my booty shorts and tube tops again," Gianna chuckled.

"I know, soon enough," I said as I rubbed her back.

As we were walking, that Shalyssa chick cut off our path. "Hey y'all," she folded her arms but stared a hole through Gianna only.

"Oh hey what's up," Gianna responded and frowned.

This girl couldn't be that damn thirsty for a fucking job, I thought.

"So I was wondering if you got a chance to talk to your man," she said to Gianna.

"Yeah I did and he said there aren't any openings," Gianna responded dryly and tried to walk around her.

"For some reason I don't believe that," Shalyssa stopped Gianna in her tracks.

Why was she so fucking thirsty for *this* particular job? There were plenty of other clubs and shit that she could work for. Maybe Gianna was right when she said she probably wanted to suck KJ's dick. That's the only reason I could see as to why she was so adamant about working at Kingin' specifically.

"Okay you need to get the fuck out of her face," I slipped in between she and Gianna. "She told you what he said, now keep it pushing," I stared her dead in the eyes.

"Nah you know what? I didn't give him your bitch ass resume. I tore it up back at the Cheesecake Factory," Gianna smiled and folded her arms.

"You could've just said you didn't wanna help instead of being a fake ass bitch," she rolled her eyes.

"No I like being a fake ass bitch, so that's why I fake gave your resume to my nigga," Gianna fake smiled as I chuckled.

"Yeah aight, karma is a bitch," Shalyssa sized Gianna up and then started to walk off.

"Is it really that serious?" I bucked my eyes.

"I guess so. But if she thought that was gonna help her, she is sadly mistaken," Gianna shook her head. "And why is she always where we are?" She turned her lip up and looked at me.

"I don't know. That is weird as fuck ain't it?" I looked back but Shalyssa was nowhere to be found.

"It's hella strange," Gianna squinted her eyes.

"Maybe we should tell the brothers," I suggested.

"I'm sure it's nothing, but you can never be too sure," Gianna nodded and then we started to walk off.

We made our way around the whole mall, and luckily we didn't see Shalyssa's weird ass again.

We left after getting some ice cream, and then I headed home so I could tell Kendrin about this girl. Like Gianna said, I'm sure it was nothing, but Kendrin told me to always tell him if something seemed strange, so I was gonna do just that. Ain't no telling what that hoe is up to, and I didn't want her doing anything to my man or his family. She seemed like the type to drug a nigga and steal his semen.

When I got into my home, I heard Kendrin in the weight room. He was working out more than usual; I guess trying to get his shoulders and abs stronger after being shot. I didn't care because he was getting finer by the minute, which I didn't even know was possible.

I walked in and he yanked me over to him to kiss my lips.

"Hi daddy," I batted my eyelashes before he went in for another kiss.

"You are so fucking pretty shorty," he bit his lip and grabbed a handful of my ass. He started pulling my dress up from behind, so I knew I had to tell him now before he dicked me down and made me forget.

"Wait baby, I have something to tell you," I said and stepped back.

"What's up?" He asked as he sat on the abs machine and began to do his crunches. Lustful thoughts seized my mind, and I licked my lips.

"This girl named Shalyssa-"

PING!

The weights of the abs machine dropped down hard as fuck, banging against one another as Kendrin stared into my eyes. Damn, maybe it is a good thing I chose to tell him about her? Her name seemed to pique his interest.

"Did you say Shalyssa?" He questioned and I nodded. "Continue," he said.

"Well she's always popping up wherever the girls and I are, and it's kind of weird. I know it's probably nothing but-"

"When did she pop up on you?" He cocked his head.

"Well once that night we went to Cheesecake Factory, and she was trying to get a job at Kingin' through Gianna. The next time was today at the mall. She was mad that Gianna didn't give her resume to KJ," I explained to him. "Why?" I furrowed my brows.

"We've been looking for her shorty. The next time you see her out, play along with whatever she's saying, and shoot me a text if you can. I will give you a location to bring her to," he said and stared into my eyes with his seaweed colored ones.

"Okay," I responded a little scared.

"Don't be scared or nothing shorty, she's harmless," he scoffed. *Then why are y'all coming for her?* I thought.

He stood up and walked over to me, then picked me up. He was so strong, but he didn't have that body builder look which I loved.

"This ass is getting fatter," he said as he put me down. He turned me around and bit my ass through the dress.

"Ah! Kendrin!" I jumped and turned around to push him lightly.

"Get upstairs, I'm about to do all kinds of shit to this," he demanded and squeezed my ass so roughly that he almost made me cum.

I didn't move fast enough, so he picked me up from behind, to take me upstairs and wear me out.

TWO DAYS LATER...

I WAS PISSED as hell for more reasons than one. That nigga TJ dragged me out here promising me the fucking world, just to slip up and get killed. I told his dumb ass on countless occasions that we were not prepared, and how we needed to take our asses back to Atlanta and plan some more. I told his stupid ass we needed to build a team, but he was sure that KJ would be no fucking problem.

To add fuel to an already burning fire, this nigga ratted me out to KJ before he died. Really nigga? After he promised me numerous times that he would never let anything happen to me, he goes out snitching like the bitch that I always knew he was. Because of him, I was now laid up in some dingy motel, which I would soon be thrown out of, scared for my life. I'd only figured out that he snitched on me because people were refusing to be seen conversing with me on the streets. When I asked why, they informed me that I had a price on my head for working with TJ. On top of that, all the people that TJ had made some sort of connection with were too damn scary to even help me hide or get out of town.

I'd heard that KJ wanted his soldiers to drop me on sight if they saw me out, and that shit had me paranoid as fuck. I didn't know the niggas that worked for him, so that meant I could be standing right next to the nigga and not even fucking know! That's why before two days ago at the mall, I hadn't been out in the open in almost two weeks. With the way I was feeling right now, TJ being dead didn't even fucking bother me. Yeah I loved that nigga but shit, he was a fucking fraud for real, and that's not the nigga I fell in love with.

Then that stupid bitch Gigi, I wanted to stomp that baby right out of her stomach after she talked to me the way she did in the mall. The only reason I even approached Gigi's ass in the mall, was not because I wanted the job obviously, but because she pissed me off by ripping up my resume. I saw her ass do it back at the restaurant, but I just wanted to see if she was gonna continue to be fake about the shit. Me approaching her in the mall backfired though, because while eavesdropping, I found out she and her ratchet ass friend were gonna run home and tell on me. I wouldn't have told them stupid hoes my real name in the beginning, had I known my scary ass boyfriend was gonna give it to KJ. But anyway, if I ever decided to go outside anytime soon, I hoped to catch Gigi alone and-

BRRNNNGG!

I jumped when the phone rang, and then stared at it. It interrupted my thoughts, and brought me back to present time.

BRRNNNGG!

I rolled off the bed and onto the floor, and then reached up to grab the phone.

PLAT! PLAT! PLAT! PLAT! PLAT! PLAT!

Bullets from a machine gun began flying into the room from the window, bursting the lamps and pillows. *I knew I shouldn't have chosen a first floor room*, I thought. I stayed on the ground screaming and crying as they riddled my hotel room. It seemed like they would never stop as I tried to lie on the floor until they ceased. Glass, pillow feathers, and pieces of broken furniture were flying everywhere as these assassins blew up my fucking room.

PLAT!

"Aaahhh!" I screeched even louder as I felt a bullet pierce my fucking calf. Hot tears immediately slipped from my eyes as the pain became unbearable.

PLAT! PLAT! PLAT! PLAT! PLAT! PLAT!

After what seemed like an eternity, the bullets stop flying in and everything became silent. I laid there panting and crying, terrified for my fucking life. I knew I shouldn't have trusted that nigga!

"I hate you TJ!" I cried out as I began to sit up slowly. "Fuck," I spat as I used the split open mattress as a crutch.

The room was a complete fucking mess as I looked around it. The TV had a big ass hole in it, and all the pillows were riddled with bullets, as well as the furniture. What baffled me is the fact that no one had called the police or anything. No front desk clerk had called to check on me and see if I was okay either. What the hell kind of city was Baltimore?

I limped to the bathroom, and plopped down on the closed toilet top so I could inspect my fucking wound. I lifted up my pants leg, and there was a big ass gash in it. It looked just as painful as it felt. I took a medium sized towel, and ran it under the hot water from the faucet. I placed it against my injury, in hopes of stopping some of the blood that was pouring continuously.

"Lord please if you help me make it out of Baltimore alive, I will never scheme or lie again," I sobbed violently as I rocked back and forth, holding my leg. I had no money to get out of the city at all. "God please don't let KJ kill me, please," I cried and dropped my head.

I WALKED into class and was surprised to see Christian. He hadn't come to class at all last week after Kendrin and KJ roughed him up. Because we only had this class two times a week, he could miss a whole week and be fine; the luxury of college.

I tried to hold in my laughter as I sat down at my preferred desk. His face was still bruised between his eyes, and his nose looked slightly crooked. He refused to look my way, and I was just fine with that. I tried to warn him that he was fucking with the wrong ones, but his dumb ass didn't wanna listen.

And thank God Kenzie had some crazy ass cousins who could do his dirty work, because we didn't want anything getting in the way of him going pro. I knew if Kenzie whooped Christian's ass, he would press charges and that wouldn't look good for Kenzie at all. However, I knew he was too scared to tattle on KJ or Kendrin, because he would end up burned to death somewhere in Frenchtown, Maryland. On top of that, KJ had a couple officers and other law enforcement workers on payroll, so he wouldn't be too protected.

"Okay please bring your paper to the front, and then you can leave. We will go row by row. Once you hand in your paper, you are free to go *immediately*," the teacher called out.

Each row started turning in their papers, and thank God Christian's row was before mine. He handed in his paper, and plodded out the classroom like a sad little child. I let out a light chuckle, and then waited for my row's turn. After handing in my work, I walked out and saw Christian leaning against the wall like he was waiting on something. I kept walking, but when I heard someone jogging behind me, I turned around to see it was him.

"Shannon give me a minute," he asked and I saw his actual eyeball was bruised. *Damn!* I thought.

"What Christian?" I huffed. I kind of felt bad for him because of how damaged his face was.

When Kenzie said Kendrin only hit him three times, I didn't expect so much damage. Then again, Kendrin was known around Baltimore for whooping niggas asses for as long as I've known him. They used to call him Scraps in high school, because he stayed scrapping with niggas and fucking them up. It was to the point where dudes would purposely try and fight him, hoping to win and gain bragging rights. It never worked though, because they always got their asses knocked out. He was such a quiet calm guy, but my dad said the quiet ones were the ones you should watch out for.

Christian was lucky I felt a little sympathy for him, otherwise I would have been walked my pretty ass to the parking lot.

"I just wanted to say that I'm sorry and I didn't mean for shit to go this far," he said.

"Oh really? How didn't you mean for it to go this far, when you were always threatening me and trying to ruin my relationship?" I cocked my head.

"I just wanted to fuck with you, but I ain't mean for you to be sticking your homeboys on me," he scowled as his eyes watered.

"Look Christian, I'm sorry that you got beat up, I didn't mean for that to happen either. I don't even think Kenzie did, but that's what happens when you fuck with people. You never know what a person has. They could have a gun, a knife, or in this case a pair of crazy ass cousins that will have you sleep in the back of the club," I said and we both kind of chuckled.

"Yeah I was scared as fuck when I woke up to some homeless woman shaking me to offer me a cup of coffee," he smiled and I laughed.

"Damn, you know you're in bad shape when a homeless person offers you something," I taunted and he cackled.

"I know right," he nodded and looked down.

"Well I hope you feel better Christian, Kenzie's cousin really did a number on you," I clenched my teeth together and shook my head as my eyes inspected his wounds.

"Yeah my mother almost passed out when she saw me. I just told her I got drunk as fuck and fell down some stairs," he said. "I ain't really trying to snitch on the Kings," he exhaled.

"If you knew about them, then why were you fucking with Kenzie?" I frowned. I was confused as hell, why play scared now?

"Because my dumb ass ain't put two and two together. I didn't realize that he may have been related to them until I was getting dragged out the club my collar," he replied and I tittered. "You think we can be cool?" He raised a brow.

"I mean probably not. Kenzie hates you, and so do Terrible One and Terrible Two," I said referring to KJ and Kendrin.

"You're right, and I know it's some more niggas in that group," he inhaled sharply.

"Oh yes, plenty," I responded and we both giggled.

"Well see you in class later this week then," he pursed his lips.

"Bye Chris," I waved and turned on my heels.

When I looked back, he was still watching me with sad eyes. I knew he liked me still, but I was happy he learned his damn lesson and was gonna leave me the fuck alone. I mean damn brother... all we did was text.

"KJ!" My mom smiled as I walked into the kitchen. She reached up to grab my face and kiss my cheek.

"Hi mommy," I smirked and she chuckled at me.

"You must be hungry, because you haven't called me that since you were four years old," she smiled.

"I was a man already, that's why," I responded and flexed my bicep muscles.

"Maybe so, because by the time you were ten months you would never let me cuddle you unless you were sleepy or hungry," she smiled.

"Told you. That's why I had to cut that mommy stuff out after four years," I smiled.

"Right. Wait no, when you were five you called me mommy just not in public," she said and we both laughed.

"Well mommy, I want a smoothie," I said and sat at the bar.

"I figured you wanted something," she replied and started pulling out the fruit, ice, frozen yogurt, strawberry sauce, and juice. My mom made the best smoothies, and they were way better than Jamba Juice and anywhere else.

"Also I wanted to talk to you for a little bit," I said as she prepared my smoothie.

"About what honey?" She questioned.

"About Gianna," I sighed and she paused making my drink.

"Problems already?" She furrowed her brows.

"You tell me. She seems very angry every time a woman talks to me," I said.

"Sounds normal to me," she chuckled.

"For real ma, like anything. She gets mad at the waitress when we go out to dinner, the valet lady, even the cashier at the store," I bucked my eyes and my mom was just cracking up.

Gianna was always protective of me, the same way I am with her, but she was never upset about people that I had no choice but to interact with, like the hostess at the restaurants.

"And she wasn't like this before?" my mom asked once she finished blending the drinks. She poured it into a glass for me, and opened a drawer. "You still want a crazy straw?" She grinned and I nodded making her laugh.

"No she wasn't like this before with waiters and shit- stuff," I corrected myself when she glared at me. Only my dad let me curse, just like he was the only one who let me say I was a real nigga when I was younger.

"Well maybe it's the baby, and maybe she feels threatened," she replied. "Especially since you have old grannies killing themselves over you. You know what? I knew I should've whooped her ass when I had the chance. She's got some nerve crawling her thirsty ass-"

"Ma! Chill on London!" I laughed and she sucked her teeth. "Don't speak ill of the dead. Now threatened? What do you mean because they don't say anything to Gianna?" I frowned and jerked my neck back.

"No baby, like she doesn't feel secure in your life right now. She feels like you could replace her any day," she explained further.

"What? I would never replace Gianna, I love her," I frowned harder because this woman shit was confusing as hell.

"Yes *you* know that, but she obviously doesn't. Maybe I'm wrong," my mom shrugged.

"So what? Buy her some shoes?" I sipped my smoothie.

"No, show her some more attention or something," she shook her head at me and smiled.

"What's so funny?" I quizzed.

"You're just like your daddy. He never knows what the problem is, and he doesn't care to find out, he just wants to fix it," she chuckled.

"What's wrong with that?" I inquired and gulped some more of my smoothie.

"Well if you don't know what the problem is, you're gonna keep doing it," she raised a brow and I nodded. "I'm not surprised that you guys are so much alike, since your birthdays are a day apart."

My father was born May 3rd, and I was born on the 4th.

"Soooo, do something nice for her?" I questioned again and she threw her head back laughing.

"Kendrick Jr., stop shooting blindly in the dark okay?" she chuckled.

"Okay what should I do?" I grinned.

"Talk to her, and not in that caveman style you get from your daddy," she responded.

"Caveman style?" I inquired and laughed.

"Yes that, *hurry up and tell me what's wrong so that I can beat on my chest about how manly I am, and then possibly get some after*," she said and I started clapping my hands while cracking up.

"Is that what we do?" I snickered.

"Yes, it's either that or the Romeo and Juliet charm you try to use," she said.

"Oh the *I love you and only you* spiel?" I raised a brow.

"Now you're getting it," she pointed to me.

I talked with my mom for about forty-five minutes longer, and had two more smoothies in the process, before my brother Kendrae and my dad walked in.

"I wanna smoothie," Kendrae pointed to the blender as we slapped hands. He sat at the bar next to me to wait.

As my mom placed the stuff into the blender for Kendrae's smoothie, my dad walked up behind her. He snaked his hands around her small waist, and began whispering some shit into her ear that had her smiling and blending at the same time. I looked at Kendrae and we both playfully scoffed.

"Don't y'all get tired of each other?" Kendrae asked.

"Look how beautiful your mother is, are you kidding me?" my dad kissed on her neck while still hugging her from behind. My mom was blushing like this nigga hadn't been her husband for twenty fucking years.

Right when the blender stopped, my dad picked my mother up from behind, and started out of the kitchen.

"Just pour it yourself baby," she pointed to the blender, talking to Kendrae as my dad carried her off to do God knows what.

"Aight, bye Drae. I got some ear plugs in my old room if you need them," I joked and he laughed while pouring his smoothie.

I left my parents' crib, and drove straight to get some roses for Gianna before going home. I was gonna try and actually listen to what she had to say, because I didn't do that a lot. Haha.

I walked into the bedroom, and she was leaning on her backrest painting her fingernails.

"For me?" She beamed when she spotted the red roses.

"Of course, who else wou-" I stopped myself short so I wouldn't use my charm that my mother spoke of.

"I would get up, but I finally found a comfortable spot to relax in," she giggled. She was wearing a big t-shirt, and her hair was disheveled, but she still looked as beautiful as ever.

"Gianna, I know you've been feeling unsafe," I said using my mom's words.

"Unsafe?" she frowned.

"Yeah, like you're not a staple in my life," I said and set the roses on the nightstand by her side of the bed.

"Oh," she said somberly, letting me know my mom's hypothesis was correct. "And baby, I lo- why do you feel that way?" I had to stop the charm again.

"I don't know. I guess because when girls come around, you don't really show me the attention that you're supposed to, you don't shut them down when they flirt, and you kind of just let me stand to the side," she explained.

"I do?" I furrowed my brows. I didn't even notice I did that shit.

"Yes, you do. Like at Target, I was standing behind that chick until you finally pulled me close," she said. "Then you were letting her touch all on your arm, while you guys gazed into each other's eyes."

"Damn baby, I'm sorry. I wouldn't like that shit either," I chuckled and rubbed her sexy thigh. "But I don't let niggas get close to you," I half smiled and so did she.

"Yes, but I'm not really in a position to do the same," she pointed to her full term but still small belly.

"I know, but I'm gonna make sure I always have you in the forefront when that happens, alright? I don't wanna disregard you baby, because I love you a lot. You mean everything to me, and the fact that you're carrying something that's a mixture of us inside you just makes me love you even more," I said. I'm sorry the charm just took over that time. Ha ha. She was tearing up by now, but she was smiling too.

"Since when do you sit and listen to me?" she flashed her perfect smile.

"Excuse me? Sixty percent of the time I'm listening when you talk," I admitted.

"Only sixty?" she slapped my arm lightly while bucking her eyes.

"Yeah, forty percent of the time I'm thinking about getting high, fucking you, and playing video games," I laughed and then put my hands up to block her little playful punch she delivered to me. "But I'm sure that's more than most niggas, shorty. Just think, with other women it was zero to twenty percent," I grinned and she shook her head. "Can I have a kiss beautiful?" I asked in a more serious tone.

"You have to come closer, I don't wanna move," she said.

"Woman come here," I pulled her gently, and then got in between her legs to kiss her soft lips.

"You're gonna mess up my nails!" she screeched and chuckled. "I love you, Kendrick," she whispered as she caressed my face.

"I love you more, Gianna," I said before sliding my tongue into her sweet mouth.

"Ооон, ииин," Aysia called out as I went ham between her legs.

Her hair was all over the place, and I smiled as I looked down at her. She bit her plump bottom lip, and pressed her small hand against my abs.

"Fuck," I moaned as I continued to beat her shit to a pulp.

I was wearing this pussy out, and you could see it all in her pretty face. Her caramel skin was red, and her face was all twisted up.

"Uuuuhh, uuuh, I'm cuuming, oh shit, oh," she cried out. Right after she said that, I felt her wet my dick, which caused me to burst all inside of her.

As soon as I did, my cell phone started going off. I had to recover from that powerful nut, so whomever it was needed to wait. I then remembered them fucking cats that were coming down from Camden, so I slowly slid my dick out of Aysia, and then grabbed my phone to answer.

"Hello?" I said into the phone.

"Aye, Lenny caught a fish and is taking it to the house," KJ spoke in code, which meant Lenny had caught a corner boy selling our stolen product.

We only spoke in code over the phone when our women or other family members were around, so he must've been with Gianna at the moment. We also used code talk if we were in public.

"Alright, I should be there to help you fry it," I replied.

"Cool, bring your own plate," he said meaning to bring my own heat. I agreed and then we both disconnected.

"Who was that?" Aysia asked still out of breath.

"My cousin. I will be back in a little bit, baby," I said before rushing towards the bathroom within our room.

"Okay, well what do you want for dinner?" She called after me.

"Catfish," I smiled and she nodded her head to say okay before standing up. I quickly showered, kissed my shorty goodbye, and then headed to the warehouse.

After parking and getting out, I put the code into the door, and then made sure it closed before heading to the torture room. I typed the code into that door, and when it lifted I saw KJ and his best friend Lenny, sitting in there with some young nigga who was crying like a newborn. If the walls weren't sound proof, you'd be able to hear his ass wailing all the way in Virginia.

"Didn't I tell you to shut the fuck up!" Lenny growled and the kid held his breath.

"Who the fuck you working for? If I have to ask you again, my boy here is gon' stab you again," KJ hissed.

My eyes darted to his midsection, and his stomach had two deep bloody wounds in it already. This nigga had better start talking so they could put him out of his misery.

"Man, he gon' kill me if I tell- ah!" the boy screamed as Lenny plunged the knife into the same wound. I cringed at the sight, and then took a seat to load my gun's magazine.

"Now, we can go all fucking day if you want to nigga! We can go all fucking day! You will bleed to death right here, unless you tell me!" KJ hollered as he paced the area in front of the little nigga.

"If I do tell you, are you gon' put me on?" he inquired and stared up into KJ's eyes.

KJ chuckled and said, "You know what, yeah. I'm gon' put yo ass on fa'sho." KJ was lying through his teeth, but only Lenny and I knew that.

"Alright umm, I'm working for this guy they call Pablo," he sniffled. "He and his homie Chef robbed the trap house and gave me some product to sell," he sniffled and then groaned from the pain.

"Pablo and Chef? What the fuck?" I frowned.

"And they only supplied *you* with product to sell?" I questioned as I continued to load up the magazine.

"Nah, two other cats as well, but I don't know their names," he responded to me and I nodded.

"Now can we get me some medical attention," he dropped his head and then picked it back up slowly. His eyelids were low and fluttering.

"Yeah man," KJ said as he slowly took the knife from Lenny, like the torture was over.

SHLUK! SHLUK! SHLUK! SHLUK!

KJ stabbed this nigga repeatedly like he was Jason Voorhees or some shit. Blood was spewing everywhere as he went ham on this nigga's guts.

"Don't you ever make me wait that long for no fucking information you bitch boy!" KJ shouted over the boy's screams as he shanked him. It reminded me of when your mother whooped you and hit you after every word she spoke.

"Kaleeini, shoot this nigga in the face," KJ ordered with blood dripping from his gloves.

"Damn, ain't he dead already-"

POP! POP! POP!

Before I could finish, KJ snatched my gun and let off three shots exploding the nigga's face. Lenny started cracking up and so did I at this crazy cousin of mine. I put my gun back in my waist, as KJ snapped pictures with some disposable camera.

"Lenny, get these developed, and when Oscar gives me the whereabouts on Pablo and Chef, I want those dropped in their mailbox. Find a courier for delivery," he told his best friend. KJ then called Bolo for cleanup.

"Bolo, take the black van and have one of your people's toss him out on the same corner where he was pushing my product. We gon' make this a fucking routine until I catch them niggas. I'm tired of these muthafuckas fucking with me, and what's a better warning to let them know that I'm coming for their asses than a mutilated body," KJ explained to Bolo.

"Got it," he nodded as he and his crew carried the fucked up corner boy out of the room.

"What was his name?" I asked KJ as he removed his gloves and lit a blunt.

"Fuck if I know. One of them cokeheads explained his looks and location to a tee for me after he bought from him," he shrugged.

"What you give the cokehead?" I inquired.

"A baggie of sugar," he said and the three of us burst into laughter.

"You cold for that," Lenny said and I nodded in agreement.

KJ shrugged with a smile before taking another pull on the blunt. "Ain't my fault he didn't recognize the shit wasn't the real deal."

APRIL 29TH

"Okay, no, I want the medicine!" I hollered as I sat in the delivery room with my legs cocked wide open.

My son was about to come, and from listening to my mother and Nic, I declined the medicine. I realized that was a big ass mistake. I couldn't do this! I wasn't strong enough. This was the scariest, most painful shit I had ever experienced in my entire life.

"I'm never having sex with you again!" I shouted through tears to KJ. He tried to kiss my face to calm me, but I shoved him back. I didn't want him to ever touch me again, especially with his lips or dick.

"Ms. Daniels, it's too late for medicine. The baby is ready," my doctor explained.

"No, just hurry and go get it! What is she doing? She can go get it!" I yelled at the nurse who was staring at me like I was transforming into the Hulk.

"Relax baby," KJ smiled as his ass went to stand behind the doctor with this big ass camera. He bought some fucking expensive ass handheld that they used for movies and shit.

"Ms. Daniels, even if we gave it to you now, the baby would come before it kicked in," the doctor said and looked at me like he was so annoyed with me.

"KJ, make them get it for me," I stuck my bottom lip out and stared at him.

"Beautiful, I wish I could," he looked at me with a sympathetic expression.

"Ahhhh!" I screamed in pain. "Fine!" I started to cry hysterically, so my mom came to comfort me. "Just know, that I know that no one in this room cares about me," I sobbed as the pain took over my body. I was soaking with sweat, and so uncomfortable.

"Gianna, rilassare, esso finirà presto, (Gianna, relax, it will be over soon.)" my mother spoke to me in Italian.

"Si prega mi ha colpito sulla testa con qualcosa di mamma! (Please hit me on the head with something mama!)," I cried to her and she chuckled before rubbing my hair back.

"Okay, let's go, he's coming," the doctor said after a few moments of silence. KJ's eyes bucked in excitement, and then he made sure his camera was on and ready.

"Aaaahhhhh!" I screamed and cried as I squeezed the shit out of my mother's hand. She didn't budge, and I was happy I wasn't hurting her too badly.

"That was great Ms. Daniels, let's do that again," the doctor coached me.

"Uggggghhhh!" I clenched my teeth together so hard I thought I was gonna crack a damn tooth.

"Okay, and one more!" The doctor shouted excitedly.

"Grande lavoro Gianna. Brava, (Great job Gianna. Bravo.)" my mother said to me as she caressed my head.

Once I caught my breath, I gave one last push, and finally I saw them lift my baby in the air. KJ looked like he was excited, perplexed, and about to throw up all at the same time. I panted heavily as I watched my mom take the camera from KJ, and the doctors instruct him on how to cut the umbilical cord. The nurse then brought him over to me, and he was so cute. His eyes were closed tightly, but I was waiting for him to open them so I could see the color.

"Okay, we want to clean him Ms. Daniels, is it okay?" the nurse asked, and I stared down at my baby for a few moments before nodding and handing him off to her.

The other nurse was cleaning me up, and I felt so disgusting. Not to mention I was in so much pain. Once she left, KJ sat down in the chair still appearing to be floored, as my mother chuckled at him.

"You okay?" I asked once I caught my breath.

"That shit was like something off of *Men In Black*," he responded while staring at the floor, and my mother and I laughed loudly.

He got up and set his mask down where he was originally sitting, and then came over to me. He pushed my hair out of my face, and then stared at me for a couple seconds. He didn't say anything as his jade green eyes searched my face. He was so gorgeous.

"You're so beautiful Gianna, and you did a great job," he pursed his lips, and his dimples were now center stage.

He pressed his mouth against mine a couple times, before sucking on my lips. I reached up to caress his cheek, and closed my eyes to relish in the moment. Our kiss was interrupted when the nurse reinterred with Kendrick III, or K-Three as people have started calling him. I hated that nickname, but everyone was already saying it so I decided against protesting it.

As she carried him to me, he was looking around at all the people in the room. "I have never seen a newborn move this much," the nurse said.

"Yes, he's moving his neck and everything. Buffo, (Funny)" my mother said.

As soon as she laid him in my arms, he yawned and then opened his eyes to look at me. I could tell he was wondering who the hell I was, and it made me laugh. His eyes were the same color as dark green bush leaves, and they were already so vibrant and bright. He was the cutest little thing I'd ever seen. All that pain and agony was so worth it.

"I have the baby picture from Mrs. King," my mother said before reaching into her purse.

Nic had given us a newborn baby picture of KJ so we could compare. She put the picture next to K-Three, and it was identical to the point where our jaws were damn near on the floor.

"Damn," KJ commented as he looked on. "And he's a Taurus just like my dad and I," he cheesed.

"Oh Lord," my mother laughed.

"You wanna hold him?" I asked KJ and he nodded.

I handed him the baby carefully, and he stared down at him with the biggest grin on his face. After a couple hours and one breast-feeding session, my friends, dad, and KJ's family showed up to see the baby.

Nic was taken aback at the sight of K-Three, and she said it was like déjà vu.

"Oh my gosh Gigi, he's gonna look nothing like you from the looks of this baby picture," Aysia chuckled and so did everyone else in the room.

"Thanks for reminding me. I did all the work," I rolled my eyes playfully.

"Now you know how I feel," Nic smiled as she held K-Three in her arms. "Kendrick, he looks just like KJ and Kendrin as newborns," she showed Mr. King.

"So crazy," Mr. King responded as he looked down at him.

"You hungry, shorty?" KJ asked me and gripped my hand into his.

"Yes, but I want Red Lobster," I smiled up at him.

"She is so spoiled because of you, KJ," my mother said in her Italian accent, and my father nodded his head.

"Do y'all see what she just went through? She deserves it!" Willow chimed in as she, Shannon, and Aysia watched the footage KJ recorded. I could hear my screams, cries, and shouts in Italian, and it made me snicker.

"What you want from Red Lobster, shorty?" KJ sighed and pulled his phone out to write it down. I gave him my order, and then he and Kendrin left to get food for me and everybody else.

I couldn't believe I had a baby, but I wouldn't change it for the world.

KALEEINI and I were coming from Lowe's, because we'd just bought some paint for the baby's room. We didn't know what the sex was yet, so we decided to just paint it yellow since that was gender neutral. We could've waited, but we didn't want to be in there painting last minute and have the fumes bothering the baby. We also didn't want professionals, because we wanted to paint the room together, like a little bonding thing.

My indecisive ass cancelled the appointment to find out the sex of the baby, because I wanted it to be a surprise now. I was hoping for a girl so I could spoil her, and Kaleeini wanted a boy because he wanted him to be the oldest sibling. Either one was okay with me, as long as it was healthy and had a pair of nice chunky cheeks like K-Three. I laughed because Gianna hated for people to call her son that, but it was the normal thing to do now.

It was around 8pm at night, and I was ready to eat and take my ass to sleep. I didn't feel like cooking, and I had a taste for some chicken from Hip Hops.

"What you want to eat?" Kaleeini asked me.

"Hip Hops, please!" I grinned at him and he shook his head.

"You had that shit yesterday," he frowned and rubbed my stomach.

"I know, and it was bomb as hell. I think Jerome was back there cooking yesterday," I said as I buckled my seatbelt.

"Who the hell is Jerome?" he questioned and sipped out the water he'd bought from Lowe's.

"I'm just saying I know it was a black guy frying the chicken that day," I chuckled.

"Racist ass. It could've been a black guy named Cody," he laughed and backed out of the parking lot.

"Yeah right. I bet his name is Jerome, or maybe even Gerald," I said and we both laughed.

He turned on some heat, and then the radio so we could listen to some music. As he drove, he took my left hand into his right one, and kissed the back of it. I just smiled at him although he couldn't see me, and then continued to bob my head to the music. He made a right, and then he slowed down and let go of my hand when something caught his attention.

"Baby, what's wrong?" I quizzed.

"Nothing shorty," he responded barely paying attention to me.

I looked around the dark and somewhat empty street to see if I could spot what had him so enthralled. I didn't see much, except for a couple bums and crack heads, and then a girl talking to possibly her boyfriend. I suddenly recognized the girl and rolled my eyes.

"There goes that bitch that was begging Gianna for a job," I scoffed. "Shalyssa, I think," I chuckled and looked at Kaleeini.

"I thought so," he responded and sped off. As he drove like a madman, he dialed KJ on his car phone.

"Hello?" KJ answered as Kaleeini hit the corner on another dark street and parked.

"I found the hoe you needed for your garden in the backyard," Kaleeini replied. *Since when did this nigga get a garden? And KJ gardening?* I thought and frowned.

"Drop it off," KJ responded.

"Right now?" Kaleeini frowned.

This had to be some code talk, because the last thing these niggas would be doing is planting shit, and Kaleeini had no garden tools anywhere in the car right now. Now I was scared as fuck.

"Yes right now. This is the only time. You know how long we've been looking for it?" KJ spat.

"Aight," Kaleeini said before disconnecting. "Get in the backseat, put the blanket on top of you, and lay down," he told me.

"What, why?" I asked as I watched him pull from the curb.

"Aysia, just do it, please," he sighed.

He stopped the car and looked at me, so I unbuckled my seatbelt and reluctantly climbed into the backseat. He looked over his shoulder to make sure I was lying down flat in his truck, and then he pulled off.

"Aysia do not get up no matter what you hear okay?" He said sternly.

"Yes," I responded and palmed my stomach. The car's speed suddenly picked up, the passenger window rolled down, and few moments later I heard,

POP!

POP!

And screams from random people. Kaleeini sped off, and I heard the window roll up in the process. I was shook up like Elvis at what I'd just listened to.

He drove for about ten more minutes, and then he said, "Come on so you can order your food." I slowly moved the blanket off my head, and then somehow climbed back up front with this belly. "You okay?" He asked me. I nodded my head yes even though I wasn't. Right now we were in the parking lot of Hip Hops, nowhere near where we just were.

After we got our food, I held the bag tightly and stared out the front windshield during the ride home.

"Aysia," Kaleeini chuckled.

"What?" I snapped my neck to look at him with my eyes wide.

"Can you please un-buck your damn eyes?" he laughed as he continued to our home. "That was an enemy that we had to get at," he explained.

"Was it Shalyssa?" I asked and he just nodded his head. "What did she do?" I quizzed. I remembered Willow telling me about Kendrin's reaction to Shalyssa, but I didn't think I'd be a witness to her getting blasted.

"She was an accomplice to some shit," he said and sipped his drink from Hip Hops. "That's all you need to know," he said and I just nodded.

After getting home and eating my food, Kaleeini ran me a bubble bath. He bathed me, and the hot water helped me calm down a bit.

"I'm sorry you had to be in the car for that, but I had to get her when I saw her," he said.

"I understand, it's okay," I caressed his face as he rinsed the soap off of my back.

"It won't happen again," he exhaled heavily.

"I said I understand, Kaleeini. I knew what type of nigga you were when I agreed to be with you," I half smiled and so did he.

He leaned in to kiss me, and I pulled on his shirt until he lifted his strong arms for me to pull it all the way off. He then stood up to remove his boxers, and then climbed into the tub with me. He gently pulled me into his lap, and I slid down on his thick and long dick.

"Mmmm," we both said in unison, before I pressed my lips against his, and began tonguing him down.

It seemed my life would never have a dull moment while dating a dope boy.

I PULLED the box out of my pocket, and then opened it to look inside before inhaling sharply and then shutting it back. After getting out of the car, I entered my house from the garage, and rushed up the stairs taking two at a time until I made it to the top. I then walked down the hall as I replayed the words I needed to say in my mind over and over again. This had to be perfect.

My watch read 2pm, so I knew Gianna was in K-Three's room, rocking him in the little rocking chair I'd gotten for her. I saw his bedroom door was cracked, and I pushed it open gently to see her rocking him like I'd predicted. Her eyes were closed, and I just had to take a picture of them. I put my phone back into my pocket, and then walked closer to her.

I reached to take my son out of her arms, causing her eyes fly open, but when she saw it was me, she smiled and then let me take him. I put him down in his crib, and stared at him for a couple seconds. I loved this little nigga and I hadn't even known him that long. Out of all the things I had done in my life, he was my greatest accomplishment. He made me love his mother more than I already did, which I didn't think was possible.

"Come with me," I whispered to Gianna.

"Okay," she said and stood up.

She was wearing a short light pink nightgown that showed her smooth light brown sugar legs. It had a deep dip in the back, exposing the tattoo on her shoulder blade, and the one in the middle of her sexy back.

She walked over to the baby's crib, and leaned in to kiss him. I could see all up the back of her gown, and her small round ass was sexy as fuck. I hadn't touched her in three fucking weeks. She turned around smiling, and moved her disheveled hair to the other side. She then lightly jogged to me, and I took her hand in mine to lead her out to our bedroom.

Once we got in there, I couldn't help but kiss her lips. She looked so pretty even though she wasn't fixed up.

"I can't yet," she giggled.

"I know baby, I was just kissing you," I said and sat her down very gently on the bed.

After seeing her push a whole human out of her body, I didn't know what was going on down there, so I didn't want to be too rough with her. She leaned back on her elbows, but then sat up once she saw me kneeling down.

"Kendrick," she whispered with her eyes wide open.

"Gianna, I know you've been waiting forever for this, and you probably thought this day would never come, but I promised you it would. I would never break a promise to you. Before I met you, I didn't think I would ever love any woman that wasn't my mom or my baby sister. I also never saw myself being with just one woman, but you changed all that Gianna. You showed me that being a man isn't only being able to pull a trigger, or protect the ones you love, but it's also about being able to show love to those that mean something to you. You've made me a better person overall, and I don't know what I did to deserve you, but I'm happy I got you baby. You make me wanna build you a house and shit. I would do anything for you, and I will always love you and protect you from any and everything that may bring you harm; you and my son. I feel like you complete me, and I honestly can't even imagine having a life without you, shorty. I don't think a nigga would be able to push on if I didn't have you as my lover and my friend. So by saying that, will you marry me, shorty?" I smiled and wiped the tears that were traveling down her face.

"Of course, did you even have to ask?" she sniffled and laughed as I slid the ring down her finger. It was a 14-carat diamond that I had to get custom made. "I guess I will put the other one on a necklace," she said referring to the yellow diamond ring I'd given her a while back.

"Yeah, because they mean two different things," I said. She chuckled as she stared at the ring, and the love in her eyes was hilarious. "What about me?" I said snapping her from her trance.

"Oh yeah, I love you, baby," she laughed and then kissed me.

Our lips parted, and I slipped my tongue into her mouth. I started standing up, and then got in between her legs on the bed. As soon as I started pulling on her panties she stopped me, and I remembered we were only three weeks into her six-week wait.

"Three more and it'll be over," she giggled. I got off of her and sat down before sighing.

I was so backed up it was crazy. I had never gone longer than three days without some pussy, and I felt like an addict going through withdrawals. I was gonna wait for my shorty to heal though, and not go out on the prowl. She'd just had my baby and that would be super fucked up of me.

I closed my eyes to gain my composure, until I felt her small hands reach up on my gray sweats. I looked down and watched her remove my dick from my pants. She took it into her mouth, and began slobbering all over it as she bobbed up and down.

"I forgot we could do this," I moaned and threw my head back. She was slurping and sucking like she was on payroll, which had me thinking about how good she'd gotten. "This the only dick you better ever put in your mouth," I said before another moan burst through my mouth. I bit my lip and palmed the back of her head, as she sucked the shit out of my dick. "Aaaah, aaaahh, shit, Gianna," she had me calling out like a bitch which I never did over head. "Oh, oh shit, fuck," I growled as I stared down at her go to work. "You gon' swallow for me?" I asked her. She nodded slowly but kept her pace. She then sped up, causing me to have to sit my ass all the way up. "Fuck, I'm about to nut," I grunted while massaging and gripping her hair. She went even faster, and it was so much spit it sounded like someone was pulling a boot out of the mud. "Uhhhh," I called out as I exploded into her mouth. She swallowed it up and licked any remnants off the head, making me shiver a little. I clutched her hair tightly in my fist, and stared down at her pretty face as she licked her full lips. "You've only been sucking my dick, right?" I frowned suspiciously, and she nodded and smiled. "You better be, shit," I panted. "I'll knock yo' little sexy ass out if you suck another nigga's dick like that," I continued to pant. She sucked the trust I had in her right up outta my dick, that's how good it was.

She hopped up once I let her hair go, and then went into the bathroom within our room to grab a warm towel. She came back out and got on her knees to clean my dick off. I rubbed her hair back as she fixed me up, and then I put my dick away.

"Can I eat your pussy?" I asked as she climbed into my lap to straddle me.

"No, not yet," she smiled. "I'm surprised you want to. Lauryn said if you watched the baby come out you wouldn't want to. Her boyfriend refuses to give head after he watched her have the twins," she chuckled.

"That's some little boy shit. I can't wait to eat that pussy again," I bit my lip and squeezed her ass gently.

She giggled and then climbed off my lap to go brush her teeth. Once she was done, she came out and smiled at me.

"I'm gonna make tacos now," she said.

See, how could I not marry her? She just sucked the life out of my dick, and now she was gonna make my favorite food.

I pulled her closer to me by her waist, raised her gown, and kissed on her stomach that was still sticking out very subtly. Even though it wasn't all the way back flat yet, her body was still so sexy to me. She caressed my head, and I did the same to her butt and the back of her thighs, while still sensually kissing her stomach.

"Damn, I cannot wait. And I haven't forgotten about our bet," I picked my head up and she laughed.

She pecked me lightly, and then grabbed her robe to go start cooking. I never thought I'd say this, but I couldn't wait to make her my wife.

A COUPLE DAYS LATER...

KENZIE'S CAR was in the shop, and since Shannon dropped him off to practice, I told her I would pick him up and drop him off to her since she'd be busy. It was my off day in a sense, so I didn't mind going to get my cousin, and ain't like he always asked me for shit. Plus, I knew he would do it for me.

Aysia was gone to Gianna's and KJ's, because she wanted to see their son and Gianna's big ass engagement ring again. I think it was her way of dropping hints with her passive aggressive ass. I laughed to myself as I thought about my shorty.

I pulled into the parking lot near the gym, and found a park in the pretty empty ass parking lot. It was around 7pm, so all of Kenzie's teammates were clearing out. I texted Kenzie to let him know I was here, and he promptly texted back that he was on his way out. A few minutes later, I spotted him walking out with a gang of bags, so I decided to help him out so that we could get the fuck out of here. I was hungry as fuck and in the mood for some Legends. I got out and jogged the little ways to the doors of the gym.

"What's up, and thanks again man. I got some gas money for you," Kenzie said.

"Nigga, put your money up," I frowned and picked up one of his bags.

As I placed it on my shoulder, a red Charger drove by, and when the window rolled down I saw it was the nigga that Kenzie had beef with at the club. He had a bruise on his eye, which I assumed was maybe permanent because Kendrin whooped his ass over a month ago.

"This nigga," Kenzie scoffed.

"Can I help you?" I frowned. I guess Kendrin breaking his foot off in his ass wasn't enough for this nigga.

A smile appeared on his face, and then the back tinted window rolled down and started firing shots.

POP! POP! POP! POP!

Kenzie and I scrambled around until we made it inside the empty gym. *What the fuck just happened?* I thought, as my body started to feel like it was on fire.

"They got you!" Kenzie yelled just as we listened to the car speed off.

I looked down, and once my adrenaline decreased, the burning sensation in my shoulder, the back of my leg, and my rib area turned to excruciating pain.

"Fuck," I said as I collapsed to the ground. Blood was coming out of my mouth, and dripping onto my polo.

"Hold on, cuz," Kenzie said as he held his iPhone to his ear.

My vision was getting blurry as fuck as I tried to nurse all three of my wounds, which were bleeding out profusely. I was doing that, all the while trying not to choke on the blood flowing out of my mouth. Blood was everywhere around me, and covering my hands, lips, and chin. I was dead; I knew it.

"Tell Aysia..." I couldn't even finish my sentence, and I doubt Kenzie could make out what I was trying to say anyway.

"They're on the way cuz, shit!" Kenzie shouted, but his voice sounded like he was under water. I started to cough up more blood, before letting my head hit the gym floor.

"Kaleeini!" he hollered and I could tell he was right on the floor next to me at this point. "Kaleeini, man come on! Open your eyes!" he hollered again and tapped my face. I couldn't move, and I could only see blurry colors. "Kaleeini!" Kenzie screamed at the top of his lungs, which echoed over the huge ass gymnasium, just before everything went black.

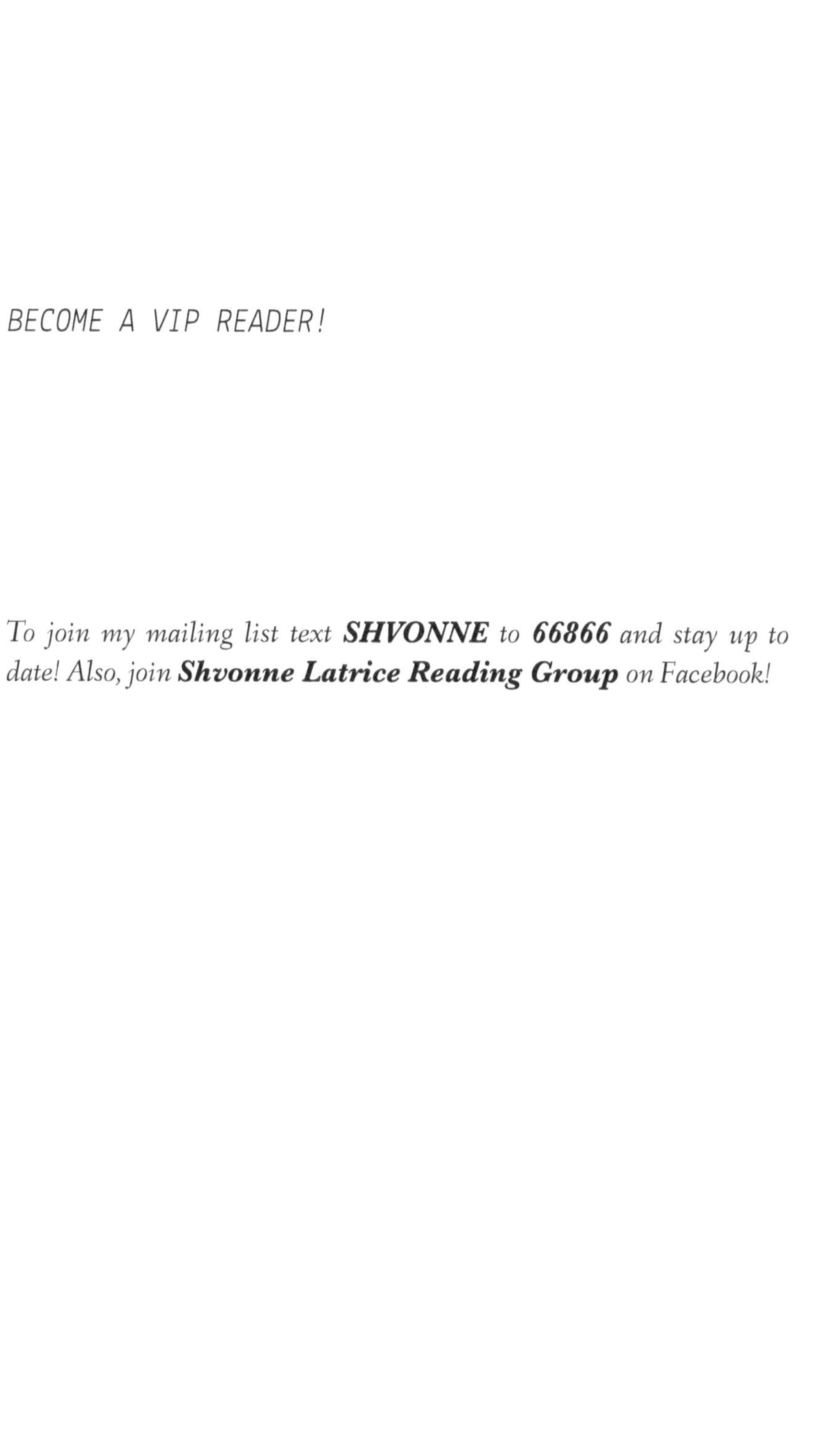